Jane Chambers'

BURNING

The author of the hit plays, *Last Summer at Bluefish Cove*, *My Blue Heaven* and *A Late Snow*, has written a tale of love that transcends time!

Cynthia desperately needed a break from the city routine and grabbed the offer of a vacation home, sight unseen. Hiring Angela, a young woman who lived in the same apartment building, to help her take care of the children, Cynthia took possession of the old New England farmhouse.

And then from an earlier century, Abigail and Martha reached out to possess the living. Cynthia and Angela helped Abigail and Martha live out the love which the latter pair could not complete in their own century, and let their spirits be set free, to rest together in eternal love and peace.

BURNING

a novel by

Jane Chambers

JH Press
P.O. Box 294, Village Station
New York, N.Y. 10014-0294

Cover design: Aenjai Graphic Studio, New York City

First published by Jove Press, May 1978

First JH Press edition, July 1983

Library of Congress Cataloging in Publication Data

Chambers, Jane, 1937-1983
    Burning.

    I. Title.
PS3553.H258B8 1983   813'.54   83-9386
ISBN 0-935672-10-9

For my life-companion, Beth, who loves *ghosties and goblins and long-leggity beasties and things what go bump in the night.*

Chapter One

It was August.

August.

Too hot for living.

"It's the pits, August in the city," Cynthia said to Dave way back in May when the one living tree on West 92nd Street turned green and glinted sunlight, forecasting summer months ahead. "If we can afford any kind of vacation this year, it should be in August."

"It's a rotten month for business, too," Dave agreed then, and buttered an English muffin, lathering it yellow, licking the drippings from around it with his tongue, "but then all months are rotten for my business."

And it's your fault.

She heard the words, although he didn't say them. He was a plodding sort of guy. He ambled through life easily, smiling in a slightly inattentive but absolutely charming manner. Everybody loved Dave; "What a nice guy!" He was pudgy as a teddy bear and just as open-armed with his affection. Like a bear, he was always slow and solid. Dave never rushed.

It was what she loved about him. It drove her crazy at the same time. Ambivalence walks hand in hand with love.

He didn't like to be pushed but she pushed him. Sometimes, when she pushed him, he balked and snarled. Sometimes, however, if he thought that she was pushing him for his own good (he considered himself a rather lazy bear), he'd plod in the direction in which she'd pointed him.

That's how he got in business for himself. Cynthia pushed. Her reasoning seemed sound enough and Dave, though he was frightened of such a financial gamble, acquiesced because it seemed to be the right thing to do at that point in his life. Dave liked to do the right thing.

The subject first came up two years before, the night of April 14th. It was nearly midnight and Dave sat in his undershirt before a battlefield of canceled checks which were spread out across the kitchen table. Occasionally licking the dull point of a pencil, he was scribbling figures on a legal pad and casting wary glances at the printed income tax form at his elbow.

"So how much did we make last year?" Cynthia cleared her throat after she spoke and looked down at the floor. Dave insisted that she refer to *his* earnings as *their* earnings but, having been a working woman before her marriage, she was never quite comfortable doing so.

"Close to twenty thousand," Dave muttered and continued scribbling.

"Twenty thousand?" It was four thousand more than he'd made the previous year, but their savings were still paltry. The cost of living, the price of meat and fuel, two kids whose *wants* expanded at the same rate as their shoe sizes.

"The only way to make money and keep it," Dave's mother, who'd been in business for herself when she was young, had once advised them, "is to make a lot of it and be your own boss."

Dave had worked for J.T. Lauder Talent Agency, a firm which supplied a large percentage of the actors and on-camera spokespersons for TV commercials. He'd worked there five years, on commission, taking as his salary ten per cent of the ten per cent the agency collected when he booked an actor.

"That means that you made two hundred thousand dollars for J.T. Lauder last year!"

Dave nodded, spit on the nub of his pencil lead and scribbled another set of figures on the legal pad.

"You're a really good agent, Dave." Cynthia always flattered her husband before she pushed him. It was a form of manipulation she'd learned from her mother.

He smiled at her, vaguely. His eyes were glazed. She knew he wasn't listening but she plunged ahead.

"If you can make two hundred thousand dollars for J.T.

8

Lauder, you can make it for yourself!" She repeated the same thought, rephrased, four or five times before he finally pushed the pencil behind his ear and answered her.

"It requires capital, opening up my own business. And you've got to have the right contacts and a stable of really good actors to survive."

"You've got the contacts. Every actor in town respects you. They'd leap at a chance to have you represent them."

"They'd leap at whoever can get them a job. My contacts are Lauder's contacts. I couldn't count on them to give me the time of day if I were on my own."

"But they like you. They like doing business with you."

Dave smiled shyly. He returned his attention to the income tax form. "Yeah, I think so. I think they do," he said, softly, modestly, but, in fact, Dave knew that he was well-liked in the theatrical industry. He was proud of that fact. On his birthday that year, his co-workers had given him a party; all the VIPs from the ad agencies and TV attended. They presented him with a chocolate cake, inscribed in sugar icing: *To the one teddy bear in a business full of snakes.* Dave had no doubts about his popularity—or his ability to sell an actor's services. He had a lot of doubts, however, about his ability to start and run a business of his own. He didn't share those self-doubts with his wife. A man has pride.

And so Cynthia, strong-headed and determined to proceed with what was good for Dave (and consequently for herself and for the kids), approached Dave's mother privately, then presented Dave with a check for $25,000 of his mother's money.

"Capital for your own business!"

He couldn't say no, he couldn't show that the thought of such a gamble stiffened him with terror. He gave notice at Lauder, rented a midtown office and, at the onset of a nationwide economic depression, he paid a painter $47.00 to letter DAVE MARTIN, THEATRICAL AGENT, on the office door.

A year and a half later, they were still siphoning off the capital to meet their living expenses. Most weeks, the business made too little profit for Dave to pay himself a salary.

On one hand, Dave was happy that he'd made the move.

9

He liked his name hand-lettered on an office door. He liked being his own boss. He reveled in the freedom and the power to tell a recalcitrant actor to get the hell out of his office or slam the phone down while a hostile ad agency exec was in the middle of a monologue. He liked not having to be so damned nice all the time. He'd gotten a taste of dignity, he'd savored it, he didn't want to let it go.

On the other hand, the business was failing. He hoped it was attributable to bad times all over the country. Everybody was broke. Businesses were crumbling everywhere. He'd read it in *Newsweek*. It wasn't him, it was the times. He'd have to hang in, hang in and hope. He didn't want to fail. He didn't want his wife to see him fail. Or his mother. He worried about his mother's money. She'd mentioned it once, quite idly, in passing, to let him know that she was depending on the repayment of that $25,000.00. "It's my ace in the hole," she said sweetly. "What if I should get cancer or something? Cancer's expensive, you know."

The money was running low and business wasn't picking up. Dave was anxious; bears get surly when they're anxious.

"August is miserable," Cynthia continued that morning at breakfast. Dave seemed to want to make an immediate reply but his mouth was full of English muffin. "The kids really need to spend some time in the country."

It hadn't worked out the way she'd planned. She'd fully expected that Dave would open his office doors to great fanfare and that, within a year or so, they'd be as rich as J.T. Lauder. She had faith in Dave. She was disappointed. She felt guilty.

Dave swallowed.

"If I was still working for Lauder, I could take a summer house on Long Island. You and the kids could spend three months on the beach." He pursed his lips and patted them with a napkin.

"You think it's my fault, don't you? If I hadn't gotten the loan from your mother, if I hadn't pushed you. . . ." She stood up suddenly and cleared the table.

Dave shoved his chair back and rose from the table, like

a caged bear. Cynthia could feel his angry presence at her back.

"That's what you think, isn't it?" She heard Dave sigh and felt his footsteps as he moved to leave the kitchen.

He paused a moment at the door. "I'm sorry, honey. We can't afford a vacation this year."

Cynthia wasn't a brat, she wasn't a spoiled wife. While she dreamed of living more luxuriously than they did at present, she had no grandiose fantasies of being rich. She was tired this year. The children were unusually troublesome—they both had colds they couldn't lose all winter. Janet had taken to playing sick, even when she wasn't, to avoid facing the mysteries of addition and subtraction. Pete had progressed from toddling to running, jumping, climbing, and couldn't be trusted for a moment out of his mother's sight. Cynthia had squeezed pennies at the supermarket every week and felt obligated to search through women's magazines for money-saving recipes. They couldn't afford their annual subscription to Lincoln Center and they hadn't had a meal out or seen a first-run movie all winter long.

She needed a vacation. A place, some time of her very own. She felt frustrated, angry at Dave for his lack of success, angry at herself for pushing him into it in the first place. She cried a lot, unreasonably. She screamed at Dave and at the kids.

"Why can't you take the kids to the zoo today? Why can't you take them to the office with you, at least? I want to paint, and Pete always sticks his fingers in my palette! I've got to have some time alone."

Dave flared in response.

"I'm trying to run a business! I can't close up and take kids to the zoo. I can't take them to the office, for God's sake; I'm trying to run a business!"

And doing a rotten job of it.

She didn't say this but he could hear it in his head, so he retaliated. "When you can make a living painting pictures, I'll see you get the time to do it. In the meanwhile, you're a full-time wife and mother. That's your job!"

By the time the long-awaited summer came, they were close to hating one another. They barely spoke. June passed in silence. In late July, their daughter Janet's bike was forcibly ripped-off from under her in Central Park. Pete was mugged at his makeshift lemonade stand outside their apartment building.

"Can't you keep an eye on him, for god's sake? He's only a four year old boy!"

A college student, named Angela, moved into their apartment building. Dave hired her to work part-time in his office.

"How can you afford to hire somebody? You can't even draw a salary!"

"If I could get out from under my desk and the phones, maybe I could drum up some business. I can't make new contacts locked up in that office. You have to spend money to make money!"

Dave's reasoning was sound but he felt guilty, anyway. He hired Angela to baby-sit on Saturdays, as well, so he and Cynthia could have time to themselves. They went to *Loew's 72* for a dollar apiece, watched B movies, and listened to the theatre's antique air conditioner leak and whimper.

Hateful. It was a hateful summer. Cynthia had fantasies of selling all the furniture and flying off to Iceland while Dave was at work. Dave was so angry at the world that he stopped rescuing stray dogs and pigeons from the traffic. An old lady got onto a bus that he was riding and he defiantly stuck to his seat.

Then, Lady Luck got on the elevator in Dave's office building. At least, Dave assumed the effeminate young actor was a lady, but Dave didn't know this chance encounter would be a stroke of luck.

He cornered the actor, Leonard Rogers, immediately, seizing the young man's forearm so he couldn't get away. "You owe me twelve weeks' commission for that job you did last spring." It was hard for Dave to ask for money, even money due him, and though Dave meant to sound harsh, it came through as a gentle request.

"I don't have it, Dave," Leonard shrugged. Dave was the nicest agent he'd done business with and one of the few who'd actually gotten him a paying job. He felt beholden.

"I haven't worked in three months and my father's been ill."

"Sure." Dave was sweating—from the ceaseless summer heat and from the embarrassment of asking for the money. "I suppose your dog died, too."

Leonard flinched. He'd never heard Dave say a sharp word to anyone before.

"Forget it," Dave apologized. "I need a vacation."

"Listen," Leonard said, brightening suddenly, "I could help you out with that."

Dave was only half-listening. He was imagining the stack of bills that awaited him upstairs on his desk. Shuffling Peter to pay Paul. He had a headache growing just above his eyebrows.

"I told you my father's been sick," Leonard continued.

Dave mumbled "Sorry."

"He's in a nursing home now. The family house is empty. It's a barn of a place on ten acres up in Massachusetts."

Dave started listening.

"It's got a creek and a pond. Terrific for kids. I grew up there."

Dave looked up at Leonard. He wasn't sure that was a plus.

"I don't need a vacation," Leonard said and grinned. "What I need is a job."

The elevator doors slid open at Dave's floor.

"Come on in," Dave said, "I'll make some calls, see what I can do. No promises."

Dave's luck held and he got Leonard two auditions for that afternoon.

"Whether I get the jobs or not, the house is yours." Leonard pressed a set of keys into Dave's hand. "That commission I owe you. . . ."

"Forget it," Dave said and shoved a piece of paper across the desk. "Just write down the directions, will you?"

And so on August 3rd Cynthia, who'd borrowed her mother-in-law's vintage Buick station wagon, loaded her kids and luggage, squeezed into the steaming bumper-to-bumper traffic of New York City and slowly headed north, Angela Lucenti at her side.

Angela's lap overflowed with road maps. A nineteen-year-old native New Yorker, Angela had driven barely enough to secure a driver's license and was wholly unfamiliar with the webs of blue, black and red lines devised by sadistic cartographers to confuse even the most seasoned motorist.

She unfolded one entitled NORTH EAST UNITED STATES and turned it a full 360°, attempting to locate the island of Manhattan.

Cynthia glanced at Angela and smiled politely. "I'm glad you're going with us."

Angela, who had at last located Bangor, Maine, and, with her finger, was trailing her way south, smiled back. "Oh, so am I. It was terrific of you to ask me. I really needed a vacation."

"It was Dave's idea," Cynthia said graciously, and it was true. The girl made her slightly nervous. Oddly, she trusted Angela with the children, and Dave said Angela did good work at the office—still, something about the girl made Cynthia wary. She felt Angela staring at her; Cynthia kept her eyes fixed straight ahead, not acknowledging the girl's attentions.

The sign ahead said *125th Street, Exit Only.*

"I have to get out of this lane," Cynthia muttered to herself. "I don't want to get off at 125th Street."

"It'll be fun," Angela ignored Cynthia's anxiety about changing lanes in heavy traffic. "We'll have such fun, won't we?"

"Yeah!" Pete said from the back seat.

"It won't be much vacation for you," Cynthia snapped. "Taking care of the two of them is a full-time job."

Angela glanced back at the youngsters. Janet was immersed in *Wonder Woman Meets The Spider Lady* but Pete was kneeling on his chubby knees, staring out the window at a massive St. Bernard in the next car.

"Can I have a dog in the country?"

"No, darling." Cynthia stuck her hand out of the window and waved frantically, a city's driver's hapless plea to

14

change lanes. She wished Angela would stop watching her every move.

"You said I could have a dog if we lived in the country."

"We're not going to live there forever, darling; we're just taking a vacation."

Cynthia smiled coquettishly at an elderly driver in the left hand lane but he glared back, quickly and possessively closing the gap between himself and the car ahead.

"Did you pack my frisbee, Mommy?"

Cynthia waved at a carful of long-haired teenage girls but they waved gaily back and made faces at the children, insensitive to her predicament.

The EXIT ONLY sign loomed larger. Cynthia felt Angela's constant gaze, and her left eyelid began to twitch. She stopped it by placing the butt of her hand in the hollow of her eye.

"Mommy, why did that lady stick her tongue out at me?"

"She thought it would amuse you, darling."

"Is something the matter with your eye, Cynthia?"

"You told me it's not nice to stick your tongue out, Mommy."

"It's *not* nice, darling. No, my eye is fine."

Cynthia turned on her directional and waved her arm again but no use. At the EXIT ONLY turn-off, she stopped dead and let the cars behind her lean on their horns until a bearded boy in a pickup truck took pity on her and provided an opening for her to enter the left lane.

The *tick-tick* of the directional, the crescendo of horns, the blue-gray tidal waves of car exhausts had already given Cynthia a headache. Manhattan Migraine, she called it, and she felt a fierce and sudden rise of excitement in her belly at the expectation of green hills and trees.

"That's the trouble with the city," she said to Angela, making conversation. "We've got no space. People go crazy when they have no space."

Angela shrugged. "I guess I'm used to it."

Cynthia, a tumbleweed from vast Montana, had never adjusted to shoulder-to-shoulder living. A fine arts major, she had grand dreams of filling canvasses with daring visions but, at the solid insistence of a practical mother, she

15

migrated to New York to study commercial art. Six months later, working part-time in an advertising agency, she met the pudgy teddy bear who was to become her husband. Blonde and rangy, Cynthia was slightly taller than Dave, but she was assertive like his mother; he was compulsive like her father, and Cupid had no trouble taking aim.

"The Meztek Indians believe that space is sacred. As soon as an infant can crawl, they ceremoniously let it loose. Wherever it sits down becomes that infant's space for all eternity. No one else will ever occupy that space."

"Until the person dies." Angela had the map wide open on the front seat, peering in its folds, trying to locate the West Side Highway.

"Forever," Cynthia said firmly. "That space is occupied forever—first by the living, then by the spirit. No one else may ever invade that particular space."

"I hope I'm not doomed to haunt a four-floor walk-up for eternity."

"Mommy, did you pack my frisbee?"

"Yes, darling."

"Here we are!" Triumphant, Angela pointed at the lower edge of the map. "And here's where we're going." She trailed her finger sixteen inches upward.

Pete leaned over the seat to look.

"Endurance, Massachusetts, just inland from Great Misery Bay."

"Those puritans were dour chaps." By the grace of God and the good will of a middle-aged woman driving a Chevrolet, Cynthia avoided being shuttled onto the access to the George Washington Bridge.

"Must be a tiny town, it's in fine print."

"Mommy, where did you pack my frisbee?"

Cynthia sighed. "I think it's time for you to go to work, Angela. He's all yours."

"You can't play with your frisbee in a car, silly." Angela turned and pinched Pete playfully on his small nose. "Now sit down like a good boy and read your comic book."

Pete sat but only for a minute. "I could *hold* my frisbee."

"I think he's going to be a lawyer." Angela said to Cynthia.

"Or a con man."

"Where is his frisbee?"

"In the bottom of the big suitcase, of course."

Angela turned and faced Pete, eye to eye. "You can't have your frisbee."

He considered that a moment. Had his mother said it, he would have stamped his feet and cried; that brought results. Angela was not so easily conquered; he turned and reached for one of his sister's comic books. "Okay."

Cynthia was startled; she'd expected several wails, at least. And she felt, oddly, a little jealous that Angela so easily subdued her son. "Don't get your hopes up, Angela, it isn't always that easy."

Angela smiled, her glance locked on Cynthia's profile as she drove. Angela had no trouble when she baby-sat, although she didn't think of herself as a potential mother and, in fact, had little first-hand knowledge of mothering. She'd been reared strictly and with gruff, reserved love by her father, a widowed taxi driver. Grown women had come and gone in her life—a housekeeper when her father could afford it, a kindly neighbor who eventually moved away, the mother of her best friend, who had a little love to spare. Even at nineteen, Angela still hungered sometimes for the warm comfort of a woman's arms and breasts, to cradle her, protect her, ready her for the strange and frightening world of grownups. She'd had a teacher in high school, a woman with a warm and caring smile, and Angela once dreamed she talked to this teacher in a way she'd never talked to anyone. She told her all her fears and asked the questions that she couldn't ask her father. In her dream, she wept and felt secure against the warm, soft flesh of the teacher's ample breasts. In reality, she never had the courage to speak to the teacher at all. She trembled and became almost speechless when the teacher called on her to recite in class.

When Angela first saw Cynthia, blonde and tall and rangy, mounting the steps of their apartment building, Pete on one arm and Pete's stroller on the other, Angela had the same, immediate, sensation. She'd heard it called a crush. Whatever one might call it, Angela was enamoured of this older woman, and the needs Angela had built up over nineteen years of life were strong.

Cynthia knew the girl was trustworthy, responsible, a hard worker who waited tables, baby sat, took typing jobs to pay her way through college. Cynthia, a farmers daughter, understood the meaning of hard work, and admired the girls grit and determination. Still, there was something about Angela that made Cynthia uneasy. She couldn't put her finger on it.

"She's so intense," Cynthia complained when Dave broke the news that he'd invited Angela to spend their vacation with them. "She keeps staring at me all the time."

Dave was flustered by Cynthia's reaction. He thought she'd be delighted to have help with the kids. "Don't look a gift-horse in the mouth," he grumbled. "She's working free."

"I can't pay you," Dave had said to Angela when he told her of the trip, "but you'll have room and board, and lots of fresh air. It's no vacation for Cynthia if she's got the kids to deal with, day and night." It was, in fact, no vacation for Dave either with the kids foot-loose. He loved his kids, but he had little patience with the noisy and exuberant aspects of their growth.

Angela had only travelled to the five boroughs of New York City; she'd seen Jersey, from the Hudson River Shore. But if she'd traveled the whole world and there was nothing left to see, she would have come on this trip. A month with Cynthia, four days alone with her before Dave joined them; this was the most exciting thing that had happened in her life.

To control the overwhelming joy that was bubbling in her, she lied politely. "Too bad Dave couldn't come up with us."

"He'll come Friday night. He has a client up for a really big job, spokesman for *Continental Coffees,* and he can't afford to take the chance of losing it."

"I'm finished with this one," Janet said in the back seat, "you can have it." She removed the comic book from her brother's hands and replaced it with *Wonder Woman Meets The Spider Lady.*

"I don't like the Spider Lady," Pete yelped in protest, "she makes me creepy."

"Janet." Cynthia warned.

"It's all right," Janet replied, *"Wonder Woman* wins."

By late afternoon, the stale sandwich from a roadside diner rumbling heavy in her stomach, Cynthia saw the sign for *Salem.*

"We're getting close."

Angela sighed softly. "Thank goodness." Pete was asleep, at last, worn out from a midday tantrum that had, as far as either woman could ascertain, something to do with the adventures of *Wonder Woman* and a lot to do with the fact that he'd had no nap.

Janet rolled a window down and struck her face into the wind, fair hair flying.

"That's dangerous." Cynthia reached back with one hand to pull her errant daughter to safety. "You know better than that. I expect more than that from you, Janet."

"But it's hot, Mommy." Janet rarely complained. She was Mommy's little helper.

Cynthia was tired and irritable, her head was splitting, and Angela was staring at her, once again. "What do you expect, it's August!"

Cynthia had written the directions on the back of a gasoline charge receipt. She would not have dared to do that if Dave had been going with them. He was a stickler for precision and neatness. He would have insisted that she print the directions explicitly, without shorthand, on an index card with, perhaps, a graphic drawing of roads and intersections on the reverse side of the card. The handwriting on Cynthia's receipt was barely legible in the growing dusk. She squinted at it.

"Tilt." Angela read, across Cynthia's shoulder. "It says *Tilt.*"

"It can't say *tilt,*" Cynthia argued and snatched it from Angela's hand. "It says *tr lt—turn left.*"

Angela took the piece of paper back. "It says *Tilt, Grimace.*"

Janet giggled.

"It says *turn left on Great Misery Road.*"

19

"Maybe I should drive and you should interpret."

"When was the last time that you drove?"

"When I took my driver's test, two years ago."

"I trust your reading more than I trust your driving." Cynthia smiled stiffly.

"I'd like to get some practice driving."

"You will, believe me. These kids will have you running into town every five minutes. But not tonight, not in the near dark on strange roads."

Angela shrugged nervously and continued to peer at the directions. "The next line looks like *pat famish*. That has to mean *pass farmhouse*."

"You're a fast learner, Angela."

"So am I," Janet piped from the back seat, "I'm in the Red reading circle at school."

Janet's proud announcement raised no adult reaction. Pete began to whimper, waking, on the seat.

The dirt road seemed to go straight up, a steep and winding incline toward the darkening sky. Thick pines, uncleared forest, tangled right and left, branches bowering the road and obscuring the view that lay ahead.

Pete pressed his face against the window to watch the dense shrubbery brush past his window.

"I bet dogs live in there."

"Dogs don't run wild any more, honey."

"I wish I had one."

The clearing appeared suddenly, a massive oval of manicured grass on the crest of the hill. Geraniums blossomed in the front yard, their red so vivid that they seemed to glow in dusklight.

Angela gasped and clapped her hands. The house was old and of weathered clapboard, but carefully and lovingly attended. Accustomed only to brownstones, tenements and an occasional visit to a two family Bronx brick house, Angela viewed it as the cover of *American Home* come to life. "It's perfect," she said and waited breathlessly for Cynthia's reaction.

Cynthia smiled and shrugged. She'd grown up in a house something like this one, isolated, aging, tended, loved. She felt she was travelling back in time to some unremembered moment in her girlhood.

She opened the rear door of the station wagon and pulled the luggage out.

"Can I have my frisbee now?" Pete tugged at the large suitcase.

"If everybody carries something, we'll only have to make one trip." Cynthia assigned Janet the smallest suitcase, hung her shoulder bag around Pete's neck and hefted the largest suitcase. "There's one left for you, Angela."

The house had obviously been cleaned for their arrival. The furniture was old, well used, in keeping with the house. Knick-knacks and pictures, ashtrays and a stack of magazines sat comfortably in place. Someone had lived in this house, enjoying it, till recently.

Janet and Pete each claimed a bedroom on the second floor, with the delight of settlers staking virgin territory. They'd shared a small apartment bedroom all their lives and had reached the ages where each had a need for separate space.

Cynthia unpacked her clothes and Dave's in what seemed to be the master bedroom. Angela watched with unreasonable disappointment. She'd slept in a room alone all her life and she yearned for the kind of dormitory closeness she imagined that two women shared in the intimacy of a bedroom. Sleepy, shared secrets. She stood by as Cynthia laid Dave's shirts in the top drawer of the largest bureau.

Tucked in the corner by the stairwell was a tiny room, barely large enough to accommodate its single bed and bureau. Angela moved her things into it, feeling as though she'd been rejected by the Martin family. "I like it," she said defiantly, when Cynthia protested, suggesting a choice among the other, larger bedrooms. "It's cozy in here, like a womb."

"Look, Mommy, the bathtub's got legs!"

Pete was crawling on the tile floor, inspecting the four clawed feet of an old iron tub.

On the wall above the toilet, Cynthia saw the patched holes where once a wooden flush box had hung, before sanitary science replaced the pull chain.

The children, hungry, headed for the kitchen. Cynthia

followed Angela down the stairs. A strange girl, Cynthia thought; she made an effort to be easy, friendly. She put her hand on Angela's shoulder. "I'll bet this house is two hundred years old."

In the practically appointed kitchen, everything was shined and spotless. Angela turned suddenly and stared.

"Look!" she cried.

At the far end of the kitchen, a door led to a small, unpainted room, so old its walls leaned inward; it seemed to be wholly dependent on the strength of the main house for its support. In the dusk, they could see that it was used for storage only, mops and brooms leaning against the occasionally parted planks, great balls of dust collecting behind stacked cartons in the corners; a startling contrast with the spotless house.

Cynthia was drawn to it as a child might reach out for a butterfly or flower, an instinctive and undeniable reaction. She stepped through the worn transom, feeling the old planks give beneath her feet. She touched the rough sawn wood that formed the walls, the handhewn beams that held the roof. Two narrow windows admitted the first rays of moonlight and the sturdy old glass panes rippled with enchanting imperfection. She thought that she had never seen such beauty. A hearth was hidden behind a pile of boxes and Cynthia pushed them back, sending a nesting spider skittering across the floor. The fireplace was blackened with soot and age, unused so long that cobwebs encrusted it in silver net.

A bed, so small it could be called a cot, was wedged into the corner by the hearth. Hacked from the trunks of cedar trees, it was fastened together with whittled wooden pegs. She reached down and pressed her weight against the frame. It was sturdy, it had withstood the test of time. The webbing that had long ago served as bedsprings dangled, rotten, frayed, from the bedframe. A chair, roughly hewn from saplings, hung on a peg above her head.

It was timeless in the darkening room and Cynthia was bound there, battered by thoughts and feelings that she couldn't focus into clarity.

22

Angela called her name a third time.

"Cynthia! There's hamburger in the freezer; shall I take it out for supper?"

Cynthia had to pull herself away, force the room to let her go. It reminded her of Pete's first day at nursery school, when he clung, crying, to her arms. She'd had to pry his fingers from her wrists and, hard-hearted, turn her back and leave him. She felt the same rush of guilt as she turned her back on the old room.

Chapter Two

"I haven't painted for awhile," Cynthia said conversationally at supper.

"Painted?"

"Painted. You know, Rembrandt, Grandma Moses."

"Oh." Angela smiled, embarrassed that she hadn't understood. In fact, she had thought that Cynthia meant *paint the walls,* something that Angela did each time she got depressed and something that the old room off the kitchen could certainly use a dose of. When she'd baby-sat for Cynthia and Dave, she'd seen no evidence of easels, palettes, even finished paintings, in their apartment.

"The room would make a perfect studio."

"That storeroom?" Angela spooned more mashed potatoes onto Janet's plate.

"Me, too," Pete said and banged his fork on his plate.

"Not until you eat what you already have."

Cynthia looked up, surprised, at the proprietous tone of Angela's voice.

Pete towed a lump of potatoes around the circumference of his plate with his thumb.

"Stop playing with it, eat it."

Cynthia was tempted to snap at Angela. "Don't talk to my son in that tone of voice," but she was reluctant to speak sharply in front of Pete. He had to respect the baby-sitter or she was useless. Instead, she changed the subject.

"I was a painter, you know." There was a note of anger in Cynthia's voice.

"Really?" Angela felt the anger, didn't understand it and stared down into her plate.

"I was serious about it. I was good."

24

"Why did you stop?" Angela asked meekly, not meeting Cynthia's eyes.

"I didn't stop. I still paint." Cynthia had not completed a single painting since her marriage. She realized, with a sinking feeling, that she had not even packed and brought her paints on this vacation. "It's hard with kids, you know."

"That old room's filthy," Angela said softly, trying to please. "I can help you clean it."

"I can clean it myself," Cynthia retorted. She didn't want Angela to set a foot inside that room. Or the kids. Or Dave. It was hers. She was drawn to it by a fierce need that she couldn't name, just as she'd been drawn, in girlhood, to the tumbledown shed in back of her father's farm. It was a private place no one would enter, a place for self, for dreams. Like the shed behind her father's farm, this room was derelict and no one would compete with her for such a space. If anyone had challenged her need for private space, she would have acquiesced. She had her share of vestigal female guilt about such selfishness. She'd had no private space, and demanded none, since her marriage.

She glanced at the old room, shyly, longingly, as a woman might glance at a man with whom she'd fallen in love but had not yet possessed. She felt as though the old room returned her longing look.

"I like the old room," she said sternly, putting Angela further in her place.

Angela was too puzzled by the conversation, by Cynthia's reactions, to continue. She shrugged and muttered, "That's what counts."

Pete spilled his milk.

The children fell asleep quite early, worn out from their long car ride. Angela stayed up, maintaining a proximity to Cynthia, hoping that Cynthia would suddenly turn warm and sharing. Cynthia, who thumbed a magazine but seemed to be away somewhere, isolated in her thoughts, grunted when Angela spoke to her, and Angela knew she wasn't being heard.

Alone in the master bedroom, the children and Angela asleep in their separate rooms, Cynthia made a list. She often made lists and always lost them, but once she'd made one, the items were imprinted on her mind. Balancing a magazine against her knee, she printed carefully in the white space above an advertisement: *canvas boards, charcoal, brushes, paints (red, blue, green, white, black, umber.)*

Dave had eked out two hundred dollars of spending money for the month's vacation. She'd have to cut it close to make it last. She ought to call Dave and ask him to collect her art supplies and bring them with him Friday, but there was a wild impatience in her and she couldn't wait. She knew he'd criticize her for squandering and he'd be right. To appease her guilt, she reread the list and scratched out *umber*.

She ripped the advertisement from the magazine and folded the page so that only her list showed. She placed it on the bedside table, patted it. Tomorrow, she would drive to town and hope she'd find an art supply store.

She snapped off the bedside lamp and lay back, staring out the open window at the glitter of stars that streaked the August sky. In Manhattan, she would be sticky this night, tossing, sighing, the only view a dirty brick wall outside the tiny bedroom window. The air conditioner would groan and sputter, victim of the city's overuse of voltage.

She breathed deeply in the pure air, letting the scent of pine and honeysuckle fill her lungs. She felt high with the expectation of adventure, without Dave directing, overseeing her activities. An explorer in a new land, she was free to wander where she pleased, free to stake a territory for her very own, a private place: the old room.

The thought of the old room, the picture of it in her mind, evoked a panorama of emotion so diverse and unexpected it flashed like wild electric sparks inside her. Her body lost its weariness, she felt light and filled with energy.

She could not lie still.

She changed position several times, she tried to think of sheep jumping fences, she counted in roman numerals, but she could not shake the old room from her; it occupied each crevice of her mind.

She surrendered and sat up in bed.

Feelings came tumbling out, one on another. She couldn't sort them out.

Happiness, a bursting happiness, the kind that comes with good news or romance. Yes, that was there.

And thankfulness, almost religious reverence for this mountain place, its sweet night air, the whooing of the owl, the muttering pines.

A fierce flush of maternal love, Pete's squalling infant face.

A chill, an unnamed fear. Pete was in danger. Something was going to happen to her son!

She shivered and tried to rise but the fear, too sharp for lingering, was suddenly gone.

She sighed, relieved.

Angela.

The girl's face flashed in quick sequence: her smile, the wrinkles at the corners of her dark eyes, the shadow of her lashes on her cheeks. Cynthia was awed, stricken by the beauty that she'd never noticed. She was caught up in the girl; amazed, delighted.

Angela's face distorted, twisted, disappeared.

Cynthia had a sour taste inside her mouth. She suddenly felt angry, jealous of Angela. She didn't know why.

She pushed her face into the pillow and tried to sleep again. Maybe she was going mad. It made no sense, this kaleidoscope of visions and emotions. She had no control of it.

Angela's face appeared again and flooded her mind.

"Damn!" Cynthia said aloud and glanced at her watch, holding it towards the moonlight. She was tired, she needed sleep.

Warm milk. Warm milk would do it.

She turned on the light, got out of bed. The floorboards were strangely cold beneath her feet.

Padding down the hallway, she felt the flash of fear again. She looked in on both the children.

Despite the summer night, Janet was swaddled in a quilt and sleeping peacefully.

Pete, the adventurer, had kicked his covers off and his plump tummy rose and fell in slow, even motions as he smiled, dreaming.

So much for midnight precognitions. Cynthia smiled, relieved.

She passed the small bedroom tucked against the stairwell and she stopped, for no reason that she knew. She turned the small brass knob and let the door creak open.

Angela slept soundly, her silhouette outlined against the window, her dark hair flowing in erratic patterns across the white pillow slip. Cynthia's eyes adjusted to the dark and she saw the faint rise and fall of the girl's breasts, the profile of her face, parted lips taking in the fresh night air. Angela moaned as though, somewhere in the magnificent dimness of her dreams, she were speaking softly to someone she loved.

Cynthia felt protective, the keeper of the house. Everyone was safe. She was content.

She quietly closed the door of Angela's room, switched on the hall light and hurried down the stairs.

Contentment left her. Her mind went wild with images. She made no sense of them; it was the kind of madness that she'd known under anesthesia, at childbirth. Faces that she knew, but not the way she knew them, features fading into one another, people out of time and out of place, events that overlapped, were distorted and disguised.

She thought of milk. A glass of milk. White milk in clear glass, she refused to think of anything but white milk in clear glass. The image tried to blur like a reflection rippled by water, but she held it tight and focused on it as she walked toward the kitchen.

She felt it when she passed the archway.

The room reached out to her, impatient, as though it had been waiting for her.

There was no need to turn on lights; she knew the entrance to the old room. Her fingers remembered the position of the cast-iron latch as though she'd opened it a thousand times.

The narrow door creaked open. She stepped inside and felt no fear. She was at home.

She could smell the cedar logs of the bedstead as though they had been freshly cut. The pine scent of the handhewn beams was new and strong. The plank floor felt firm and solid under her bare feet and she moved across it easily to the hearth, drawn by the thick and fertile odor of potatoes roasting on an open fire.

She somehow knew there was a splintered plank on the west side of the hearth and she sidestepped it as though it were a daily ritual.

It was difficult for moonlight to penetrate the warped and dirty glass panes of the windows, and it was dark inside the old room, yet Cynthia saw it all quite clearly in her mind:

An oak table in the corner, flanked by two chairs made out of saplings;

A small stool, intended for a child, sturdily constructed to withstand the wiggling impatience of youth, its rungs scraped and damaged from the climbing and kicking of small boots;

The rough-hewn bed in front of the hearth served as a sitting place in daylight, a resting place at night;

A small, handquilted pallet, folded neatly at the foot of the bed, sleeping quarters for a child.

This one room was her home and Cynthia knew its every creak and cranny, every plank and beam, as though she'd watched the trees felled and hacked into the boards that formed its walls.

A sampler, painstakingly embroidered in yellow and pink threads, hung on the wall above the table. She remembered taking every stitch, snowbound for days, the world outside sparkling and insulating her from harm.

Let him without sin cast the first stone.

She recalled the carefully stitched letters on the sampler, and an overpowering chill shot through her; she shuddered, her breath shortened, her stomach grabbed like a ready fist. She crouched, as though to strike back at a fierce intruder.

She heard a dog bark, swift and sudden warning. It had meaning to her, she didn't know just what, but she was rigid with her fear.

"Are you all right?"

Light fell across the room, and centuries vanished.

The packing crates were stacked again, cobwebs of reality once more criss-crossed the room.

Angela leaned through the doorway, puffy-eyed from sleep.

"I heard you puttering around down here and I was worried. Are you all right?"

Cynthia couldn't turn and look at Angela, not for a moment. She'd travelled too far, too fast.

"I'm fine," she said at last, and came out of the darkness, avoiding Angela's inquisitive eyes. "I thought I heard a dog bark."

Angela wanted to reach out, to touch Cynthia, to say "Whatever's wrong, don't be frightened, I'm here," but she was afraid to try to help, afraid that Cynthia would pull away, her eyes cold, and reject her.

Cynthia opened the refrigerator, spilling light into the room.

"Maybe Pete's right. Maybe there are wild dogs loose around here. I'm famished. Want a glass of milk?"

"No thank you."

Angela had the feeling she was intruding and she started to the kitchen arch.

"Wait, I'll go up with you." Cynthia poured the milk and took it with her, leaving the kitchen dark, so dark that the old room, leaning shakily against its side, seemed to disappear.

Cynthia didn't drink the milk. The instant that she lay down on the bed, she slept soundly, and she had no dreams.

Chapter Three

The doorbell rang early, so early that even the children were still asleep.

Angela pulled her cotton robe around her and stumbled sleepily down the stairs, clutching the handrail for support.

"I woke you up."

It wasn't an apology and the young man grinned infectiously. Muscular, red-bearded, he didn't wait for invitation, he simply sauntered inside, into the living room, as though he were a resident.

"My name's Roger Richmond but everybody calls me Red." He sat on the sofa, fingered his pocket for a cigarette and lit it, the acrid smell of smoke knifing the unstirred morning air. "Hope everything's all right. Leonard called from New York and asked me to get a local woman to come in and clean up for you."

Angela, still close to sleep, left the front door standing open and tagged after the visitor as though she were a lost pup.

"Don't suppose you've got coffee on yet." He grinned and sat down on the sofa. "I could use a cup of coffee."

Angela shook her head, hoping to sling sleep away and clear her mind.

"What time is it?" Her voice cracked.

"It must be after seven."

"Seven o'clock in the morning?" Angela surrendered, yawned and sank into a chair.

"Around here, everybody gets up early."

"I'm from New York City." Angela said with pride, an explanation for her sleepiness.

"I grew up in a city, too. Boston." He said it conversationally, ignoring her obvious inability to focus. "I used to wake up to garbage cans at five a.m."

"I can sleep through anything. Garbage cans, fire engines, gang fights. . . ." She listened to the sound of her own voice. It came from someone else, she was sure of that; her mind was not engaged in the words that she was hearing.

Cynthia stepped carefully down the stairs, rubbing her eyes. Pete, in underwear that hung at half-mast, was hot on his mother's heels.

"Hi." Red grinned and stood politely. "I'm Red Richmond, your nearest neighbor. Live at the foot of the hill."

Cynthia nodded wordlessly.

"Just came up to check in and see that you folks have everything you need."

"We're fine," Cynthia replied hoarsely, "I need some coffee." She headed directly down the hallway to the kitchen.

"I'm glad to hear that." Red hoisted Pete beneath one arm, passing Cynthia with long strides and depositing himself at the formica table. Pete squealed throughout the ride, too shrill a noise for the still and early hour; Cynthia winced.

Angela stumbled slowly after them, her hand feeling the hallway wall for guidance.

"Whose kid are you, Butch?"

Pete was gleefully straddling Red's knee.

"My name's Pete. That's my Mommy."

"My name's Cynthia," his mommy said as she filled the coffeepot with water, "my husband, Dave, is coming up to join us on Friday. And that's," for a moment the girl's name escaped her, "that's Angela."

Angela clung to the moulding of the archway, her eyelids still half-closed. However, super-sensitive to Cynthia, she felt the slight.

"I'm the babysitter," she said with no pride.

"I want some Wheaties!"

Angela shifted her gaze and glared at Pete. All her strength went into holding up her eyelids.

"Do we have any Wheaties, Mommy?"

Cynthia opened the cupboards, one by one. It was an effort.

"No Wheaties, darling. Angela will get some in town today."

"I'm hungry!"

"I'll fry an egg for you."

"I don't like eggs."

"You liked them yesterday."

Cynthia opened the refrigerator and selected two handfuls of eggs. She cracked them fiercely on the edge of a green mixing bowl and grimaced at the sound. She could feel the presence of the old room as she stood close by its door but it didn't pull at her this bright morning. She simply felt it there as one might feel the subsurface movement of a healing wound.

"It's a great old house, huh?" Red took a brief sip of coffee and it stung, hot, against his lips. "Ow." He blew on it, the force of his breath stirring the curly tendrils of his mustache. "My family has a cabin down at the foot of the hill. I've been coming up here summers all my life. My old man's going to retire next year and move here year-round. They're on vacation now, their thirty-fifth wedding anniversary. Hawaii." Red sang a few bars of *Aloha* but no one smiled. "I've always liked this old house, used to visit up here when I was a kid. Mr. Rogers took pride in this place and kept it up. I felt real bad about him."

"He's in a nursing home?"

Cynthia dropped the egg into the heated pan and watched it spread, hissing as the white bubbled and withdrew from the scorching metal. She wondered if the egg felt anything, fear, perhaps, or pain.

"Tall Pines. It's the best home in the state, so they say. His daughter couldn't take him, she lives out in California, and you know his son's an actor in New York. That probably means *broke*." He smiled again to no response. "I don't imagine either of them want this house so I guess it'll go up for sale this fall."

Cynthia pushed the fried egg, its yolk broken and running, in front of Pete. He wrinkled his nose.

"Ug."

"Eat it." Cynthia didn't have much authority in her early

morning, cracking voice. Pete took the butt end of his knife and printed his name across the plate in egg yolk.

"Good place to raise a family, this house," Red grinned. "I'd buy it myself if I found the right girl."

Angela, slowly awakening, felt his amused gaze, provocative, flirtatious. She knew she should be fixing food and feeding children, but she still smarted from Cynthia's forgetting her name; she pulled her robe around her tightly, more self-protective than defiant, and lightly changed the subject.

"How old is this house?"

Red looked around the room. "I'd say it was built in the 1700s but it's been renovated and expanded since then." He tapped the wall beside him. "Wallboard. This room was redone in the last twenty years."

"The 1700s?"

Cynthia glared at Angela, dawdling in the doorway, and felt put upon. She sat, cut a piece of egg, speared it with a fork and pushed it at Pete's face. He sneered.

"The storeroom on the back," Red pointed to the old room beyond the kitchen, "predates the rest of the house." He stood up and deposited Pete on a chair. "Eat your breakfast, Butch."

"Pete, my name's Pete.

"You heard the man," Cynthia said, poking at Pete's closed lips with the forks, "eat your breakfast." Angela was lounging; the strange man was heading disrespectfully into the sanctity of the old room; Cynthia was threatened, and she put a fierce look on her face.

Red fumbled with the cast-iron latch and swung the door wide open. Even in the morning light, the room was dim and filled with shadows. The smell of must and cobwebs, released, swept slowly into the kitchen. Cynthia heard Red step onto the old floor boards. They creaked and she wanted to cry out, protecting them from a careless stranger's heavy steps.

"I wonder why they never cleaned that room," Angela said, pouring herself a cup of coffee. "They kept the rest of the house immaculate." She looked at the old room and wrinkled her nose in distaste.

Cynthia saw the look. Now, she thought defensively, she

thinks I'm going to make her clean the room. Some help she's going to be this summer.

"It was just a storeroom." Red touched the old beam above his head, dragging his fingers across the ax marks.

A soft breeze from the kitchen window cornered, entered the old room and caused the cobwebs on the hearth to swing like small lace curtains.

"Mrs. Rogers didn't clean, you know. She was arthritic most of her life. They always had a cleaning woman. It's hard to find good household help, even around here where work of any kind is scarce." He tugged at the moulding around the narrow windows. It loosened and Cynthia shivered as though he'd touched her in some private place. "Mrs. Rogers died when I was just a kid, about Pete's age. I remember the funeral. August and hot as hell. I never saw Mrs. Rogers wear lipstick but they put lipstick on her for the funeral. Funny how things like that stay with you. Mr. Rogers lived here alone after the kids left home. He loved the place."

Red made a fist and rapped the weathered wooden walls. The whole room seemed to shake and Cynthia sat upright as though someone had struck her.

"Don't knock the house down." She shoved a piece of egg between her son's pursed lips.

"This room is small. Maybe a storage shed, or it could have been a keeping house for livestock."

"It was somebody's home." Cynthia said harshly, no doubt in her voice. She turned to look at Red and Pete spit the bite of egg back on his plate.

"Somebody lived here, huh?"

Red leaned against the doorframe, cocky, grinning. He thought it was a joke.

"Yes."

Cynthia glared at him as though they were engaging in a test of wills.

"How do you know? You got a ghost?"

"Ghost?" Pete squealed and slammed his fork on the plate. Angela walked over to him and took the fork out of his hand. He looked up startled for a moment, then he wailed.

Cynthia snatched the fork from Angela's hand, returned

35

it to her son, then got up and stalked to the stove, leaning against it, staring out the window.

Pete slammed his fork against his plate in steady rhythm as Cynthia poured a cup of coffee with shaking hands and stared into the blackness in the cup, the steam rising, clouding, caressing her face. She felt like crying and she didn't know the reason.

Red cleared his throat uncomfortably and tapped the old beams again. He felt he should say something.

"Beams are solid, hand hewn. Some poor fool spent a year, I bet, hacking and sawing to build this shack."

Angela shivered. She knew that Cynthia was displeased. She concentrated on cutting the egg into small pieces on Pete's plate.

"Probably some migrant put this place up, maybe a crazy hermit."

Cynthia stared into her coffee cup, wordlessly, gritting her teeth. She pondered her own reflection in the tiny pool of coffee. She knew a woman had lived in the old room.

Pete, feeling the intensity that filled the kitchen, opened his mouth, allowing Angela to fill it with a piece of egg. He chewed and his eyes darted from adult to adult.

"Good boy."

Angela stared past Red into the old room and watched a giant dust ball drift lazily across the old plank floor.

Janet, awake and fully dressed, came in, scattering the tension. She carried a massive box of multi-colored crayons and a coloring book.

"Can I have a glass of milk, Mommy?"

"You're big enough to get milk for yourself, dear."

"Don't spill it," Angela warned as the girl opened the refrigerator.

Janet poured it carefully, feeling both women watching her, replaced the carton, and sat at the formica table, spreading her coloring book and crayons neatly before her. She concentrated all her efforts on a yellow bird with one half-colored purple eye.

Pete leaned over confidentially. "They don't have any *Wheaties.*"

A sudden gust of morning wind created a cold draft that ran the full length of the kitchen and whisked into the old room, wrecking havoc with the cobwebs and dust balls. The room shivered in the draft. A covy of small dust balls, sucked from behind a carton, spiraled through the air, to collide with the wall and with each other; a massive cobweb, let loose from one side, soared silver as it piveted and clutched for safety to the ragged windowsill. A flurry of inanimate activity took place within the room: boxes, piled on one another, teetered, old newspapers rattled, a loose shutter on the outside wall slammed repeatedly in tantrum.

Cynthia knew the man must leave. "Close the window, Angela." Cynthia said suddenly; she turned sternly to face Red's hulking form, filling the doorway.

"Thank you for coming by, but everything seems quite in order."

Red raised his eyebrows, jammed his hands into his pockets and crossed the kitchen floor. Angela closed the window and the old room seemed to settle, sigh.

"If you need anything," Red, feeling very awkward, forced a grin, "just holler. I'm at the bottom of the hill."

Cynthia nodded, curtly, forced a polite smile.

Red looked past her, seeking Angela's attention. "Say, you like horses?"

"*I* do!" Janet looked up from the yellow bird with excited interest.

Red ignored her, fixing his stare and smile on Angela.

"I'm a city girl," Angela replied. "I never rode a horse."

"I could teach you," Red offered. "The farmer on the main road's got horses for hire. It's pretty countryside."

Angela glanced at Cynthia, hoping, as a child might with its mother, that she'd say No. Cynthia leaned against the kitchen sink, observing but not seeing Angela.

"Thanks, anyway. Horses don't turn me on."

"They turn *me* on!" Janet was up, tugging at Red's sleeve.

Red was as nice a guy as the next, but he hadn't planned to spend his summer as nurse-maid to a little girl. He grimaced, felt somehow cornered and patted Janet's blonde head.

"If I have time, sugar."

Janet squealed and grabbed his hand. "Mommy?"

Cynthia didn't trust the young man. She didn't know why, she didn't understand it, but she didn't like him.

"We'll see, darling, we'll see."

"Sit down and eat your breakfast, Janet." Angela was taking control of the children, and, for the first time, Cynthia was grateful. "I'll take you swimming this afternoon and we'll go exploring in the woods. Won't that be fun?"

Janet sidled back onto her chair and concentrated on the purple eye. Her lip trembled and she pressed so hard her crayon broke but she didn't cry.

At the front door, Cynthia watched Red amble slowly out of sight, disappearing in the thickly wooded hillside. For the first time since she'd awakened, she felt the warmth and beauty of the day.

"You can find the pond but don't go in it," she heard Angela instructing the children in the kitchen. "Okay, go."

Like racers at the brief blast of a starter's gun, the kids were gone, the screen door banging, bouncing to cheer them on.

Cynthia returned slowly to the kitchen. Angela was washing dishes, her eyes focused on the kids beyond the window. Cynthia pulled a dishrag from a hook and began to dry.

"Sit down," Angela said, "this is my job, remember?"

Cynthia shrugged, replaced the dishrag and paced slowly across the kitchen floor. Once, twice, three times. Angela felt an inward shudder with each footfall, as though she were doing something terribly wrong and had no idea what.

The pacing stopped and Cynthia was standing at her side. "You're making me feel guilty," Cynthia said and snatched the dishrag from the hook again.

Angela was panicked, though she didn't show it, the kind of panic that permeates, disables, when pleasing is terribly important and everything you do to please is wrong. "Well, dry the dishes then," she said, and she could hear the shaking in her voice.

Cynthia put the dishrag back onto the hook. "The hell with it, that's why I hired you."

Cynthia was aware she was being irrational. She was embarrassed, angry at herself and, consequently, angry at the nearest person. She had the feeling she was shattering, coming apart, and if she acted meanly enough, someone would save her. She wanted to scream.

"Suit yourself." Angela stiffened and her voice was shrill. She dropped a washed plate in the drainer and it rolled against the frying pan, a ringing sound.

"Be careful. We have to pay for breakage."

Cynthia sat at the table and traced the muted design of the formica tabletop with her fingernail. "I certainly hope you're not attracted to him."

Angela stopped, her hands immersed in dishwater, torn between the nasty tone of Cynthia's voice and the staggering high hope that Cynthia cared about her.

"He's pushy," Cynthia said dramatically, "and I don't trust him."

Angela, fingers trembling, lifted another plate out of the water.

"I brought you up here to help me, not to run off and have a summer romance." Jealousy. Cynthia heard it in her voice and stood up, startled.

The plate slid out of Angela's grip, spun to the floor and shattered. Angela burst into tears, fell to her knees and began wildly picking up the pieces.

The anger inside Cynthia evaporated instantly. She was desperately ashamed of her behavior; she knelt beside Angela and stopped her frantic hands from picking up the broken crockery.

"Don't do that, Angela, you'll hurt yourself." Cynthia's voice was soft and concerned, but Angela, terribly confused, could not stop crying. Her back heaved, her sobs reverberated through the room.

"Don't worry about it." Cynthia put her hand on Angela's shoulder. "It's just a plate."

"I'll pay for it!" Angela's voice nearly was a scream.

"Don't be silly." Cynthia rose and reached inside the old room for a broom. She led Angela to a chair and returned to sweep the broken pieces into a pile beside the sink.

"I'm sorry," she said as she swept. "I don't know what's wrong with me. I don't usually act like this, I really don't. Good old stable Cynthia, predictable and dull. It must be something in the air."

She looked at Angela and smiled apologetically. Angela forced herself to smile back, though tears still ran out of her eyes.

"I feel like a volcano," Cynthia continued as she got a dust pan and knelt to hold it on the floor, "everything inside me is simmering, ready to erupt." She swept the pieces in the pan. "If this keeps up, you may all have to run for shelter." She laughed, nervous, uncomfortable. "Or maybe I should do the running—to a shrink."

Angela wanted to go to her, to comfort her, to say "I understand," but she didn't understand and she didn't dare go to her.

Cynthia whistled as she dumped the broken pieces into the garbage can beneath the sink, ceramic clatter. The notes she whistled were simple, nearly tuneless, but they were familiar to her though they had no words or name.

"Whistling girls and crowing hens always come to some bad end."

Cynthia unpursed her lips and smiled at Angela. "I haven't heard that saying in a long time. My grandpa used to say that."

Angela sat silent for a moment, her forehead wrinkled. "I never heard it before."

"You must have. You just said it."

Angela shrugged. Maybe somewhere, long forgotten, in her childhood. She said it again, listening to each word. *Whistling girls and crowing hens . . .* It didn't sound like her voice, she thought, puzzled, as each word issued from her lips; it didn't sound like her voice at all. And Cynthia kept whistling that tune.

"What's the name of that?"

"What?"

"That song you're whistling."

Cynthia whistled it again, the same eight bars. She laughed. "I must have made it up. It isn't very good."

Angela, who'd had no feeling before for the old room that clung to the side wall of the kitchen, felt it watching them. Its gaze was curious and warm, perhaps a little wistful, not frightening at all. She felt a casual familiarity about it, the same comfortable feeling she had about her fourposter bed, the one she'd grown up sleeping in and had taken with her when she left her father's house to find her own apartment. She knew that bed, they were old friends. She felt the same way about the old room and there was no distress in the feeling. She was glad, in fact, and joyful. Things seemed all right now between herself and Cynthia. That brought her great relief. She wondered if Cynthia could sense her adoration, could read the fantasies that filled her mind. She hoped Cynthia's irrational behavior was not due to the "crush." Angela thought of her attractions to older women as "crushes", although she never spoke the word aloud and never acted on the feelings. She only hoped to bask in the nearness of her idols and their smallest, most inconsequential attentions to her filled her with giddy delirium. She had not the courage, or the knowledge, to expect more.

Cynthia was overwhelmed with freedom. She didn't have to wash the dishes, watch the children, plan their lunch, prepare dinner, wait for Dave's arrival to discover the structure of their evening. No one demanded anything of her this day, no one expected her to behave just as she did the day before. She'd never eaten sauerkraut before she married Dave. He loved it and she learned to halfway like it, too. She'd eat no sauerkraut this day. Her distrust of Angela had vanished. Their confrontation had seemed to clear the air. She smiled at the old room and thought about her carefully printed list on the bedside table. She would drive to town and buy her paints, set a canvas before her at the narrow window and, undisturbed by her husband or her children, she'd bare that secret place within her where the unformed dreams were hidden.

She'd be isolated, safe, in the old room.

Chapter Four

The children quickly found the pond, a placid, dark blue body of water afloat with yellowed pine needles and fed by a chilling mountain spring which spilled, at the far, down-hill, side, across a crest of rocks to become a rapid-flowing creek. Nothing would do but that Angela must take them swimming.

"Hold Pete's hand and don't let either of them go above their heads." Although Angela swore she was a swimmer, Cynthia was always nervous when the children played in water. They'd taken lessons at the West Side Y and both could float, tread water and do a passable breast stroke.

"I'll watch them every minute," Angela called as she ran with the children toward the pond. "Go on, Cynthia, have fun. It's your vacation."

The two-lane road to town appeared familiar to Cynthia and she drove it easily, somehow knowing that a clump of wizened birch would appear around one bend, a massive and gnarled apple tree would hang heavy around the next. She seemed to recognize the native landmarks as though she'd travelled this way before. Only the billboards and road signs were unfamiliar—but when she entered the small town, adrift in body shops and filling stations, she became any city slicker bewildered by the small town maze.

That was the one good thing about New York, she thought as she hesitated at each corner, staring at the street signs; the city streets were numbered, unlike these rough-paved roads entitled *Red Maple Drive* and *Pasture Hill Road*. In the biggest city in the country, you could always find your way around—here in the boondocks, you could lose your way in minutes.

She parked on what appeared to be the main drag and found a hardware store whose patched glass window displayed a dusty, minimal supply of artist's needs.

"I only got one canvas board, m'am," the bespectacled shopkeeper apologized, "only one left."

"There must be a lot of artists here," Cynthia said, on one hand disappointed and on the other happy that circumstance was going to prevent her from spending too much.

The shopkeeper disappeared in the back room and returned, blowing a cobweb off a graying piece of canvas board.

"Bought these six years ago when Miz Taylor's second kid got it in his head to paint some pictures. He was right good, too, until he made the football team and gave it up." He held the canvas board aloft for her inspection. "Too dirty for you?"

Cynthia hesitated.

"I'll give you a quarter off," he dropped it in a large brown bag, "what else'll you be buying?"

Slightly disheartened, Cynthia narrowed her list (she'd forgotten to bring it, of course, but she saw the neat printed words inside her head). The bill came to seven dollars and eleven cents; Cynthia got smug. She'd thought it might cost as much as twenty. Joyous and self-righteous as the TV housewife whose floor does not turn yellow, Cynthia paid, counting out each of the eleven cents into the shopkeeper's wizened palm.

She packed the bags under one arm and patted them in place. It was more than Rembrandt ever had, and he'd done pretty well.

The grocery list had been scrawled on the back of an envelope in Angela's fine, slanted hand; Cynthia entered the narrow, cluttered aisles of the local A&P. She bargained shopped, as Dave urged that she do at home, comparison pricing, straining to make sense of weights versus prices, considering the date on perishable products. There was no joy or satisfaction in this for her; it was a chore. Given her natural bent, she would select items that pleased her until the money ran out. But Dave, she knew, would check the prices on the cans when he arrived, and she'd be expected to remember that *Mrs. Potter's* fish sticks, which she bought, were only 69¢ and *Better Kitchens,* the next lowest priced, were 72¢. He would beam and say, "You saved three cents" and she'd feel like a dog who'd fetched the paper; her instinct was to wag her tail. The sense of freedom that had bouyed her that morning left, and reality settled uncomfortably around her shoulders. He knew their budget to the penny and she would have to account for it even here.

She felt eyes, dozens of them, staring at her. She glanced nervously around. An old lady blushed, then looked away politely. A small child grinned at her as though she were a creature in a zoo. An overalled worker eyed her appreciatively, young mothers darted quick, embarrassed looks across their gorged shopping carts. She was a strange face in a small village and she could hear their unspoken questions. *Who is she? What's she doing here? Somebody's relative from out of town?* The village had no tourist attractions, a new face had one of two meanings: a relative's in town (one of us is dying) or a new family has come to live among us.

Cynthia smiled warmly, hoping to assuage their fears. At the check-out counter, she introduced herself loudly and heard a relieved tremor pass among the curious customers.

"We're vacationing for a month at the Rogers' house."

The checkout clerk, a girl with pimples, efficiently rang up the items. "I know that house," she said matter-of-factly, "My Grandma used to work up there. Didn't like it much, but there's not much work around here, you got to take what you can get."

"She must have been the housekeeper."

The girl nodded and pushed a gaggle of canned goods past her, sending them to crash against the far end of the counter where an adolescent boy tossed them into a bag.

Cynthia felt a flush of anger at the girl, a peculiar loyalty to the house and to the Rogers. "I understand the Rogers were nice people."

The girl looked startled. "Oh, yeah, nothing wrong with them. It was the house gave Grandma the creeps, especially in the summer. She always saved her time off till

44

August and took it in a lump. She said that place was weird in August."

The bagboy laughed, the high-low giggle of a teenage voice.

The clerk sighed, turned to him. "Sit on it, Chip."

As Cynthia paid, the girl said "Red Richmond find somebody to clean the place up for you? He was in here last week, asking. Grandma won't do cleaning anymore, not since she broke her hip last winter shoveling snow."

"I guess he did; the house is clean."

"Probably Miz Hughes, I told him to go by and ask her. She needs work since Buddy lost his job."

Cynthia didn't ask who Buddy was, she didn't care. The bagboy, already jowly in his late teens, stacked the overflowing bags and hefted them onto his hip.

"Where's your car, lady?"

"The old wagon, right out front."

Sputtering, still giggling, he carried the bags out to the car. The teenage checker looked at him through the plate glass window and stuck her tongue out.

Cynthia was still offended by the casual familiarity the checker had shown with the Rogers house. The girl's attitude invaded Cynthia's sense of privacy.

As the boy loaded the bags into the wagon, Cynthia reached quickly for the adding machine tape. She slipped it in her wallet. Dave might want to see it. It wasn't that he was an ogre, demanding that she account for all the household money. It was, in fact, a kind of game. She'd seen other married couples play it, too. The husband, knowing that his wife was clearly in charge of the household, blustered and nit-picked at her expenditures. "I'm the head of this household, I pay the bills," Dave would say, perusing the grocery list, "I have a right to know where the money's going." It was all for show, a flashing of male peacock plumage, and though it irritated Cynthia, she didn't take it seriously. She placated him by showing him the bills and when he chastised her for spending too much, she remembered the evening she'd overheard him tell their son, "Be glad you're not a girl, Pete. You'll never have to have a baby or do the grocery shopping."

"Listen, lady," the bag boy interrupted her train of

45

thought. He grinned, puffing up his small jowls. "You need any yardwork done up there, you call on me. I got my own electric mower and hedge clipper."

Cynthia smiled, disinterested, and nodded.

"And I'm not scared of ghosts." He slammed the rear door shut and snorted. She dropped a quarter in his hand. "Thanks, lady." He laughed again, high-low, and jogged back into the store, his long white apron caught between his legs and flowing out behind like a bushy tail.

The unpaved road that led up to the house was dusty this dry August; through the particles of dirt that clouded the windshield, Cynthia saw a golden expanse of flowering weeds beyond the pines. Somehow she knew it marked the entrance to the creekbank. So far away she could hardly see the individual flowers, she still seemed to smell and recognize the place, the tickle of thick pollen filling her nostrils, the titillating thrill of running naked along the creek, toes squishing, disappearing in the thick, dark mud.

Cynthia had run naked along Montana creek banks in her girlhood, and she rationalized that this sudden catapulting out of reality could be attributed to fond memories. Still, she had no way of *knowing* that the creek ran downhill at that spot, hidden by wild flowers.

She smiled and shrugged. Perhaps it didn't.

A covy of quail, towing their young, darted across the roadbed; a cardinal, brilliant as fire, flashed from tree to tree following its protective mate. The birdsong and the morning wind, whisking in short, soft spurts across sunburned wild grass gave Cynthia a heady feeling, open, glorious, the sustained pitch of excitement borne by a woman in love.

The house was empty, Cynthia was glad. She stood in the kitchen, letting window-filtered sunlight warm her body as she sorted out the groceries, selecting a cupboard for one sort of goods, an undercounter cabinet for another. It was a chore she usually hated, but she felt joy, then, alone in the kitchen, finding space to store food for her family. She took her time, reading the labels on the cans, considering the recommended recipes. She felt important, the provider, and, for a moment, envious that Angela was sharing her

46

protective woman's role. So small a part of life these days, she thought, was spent in shopping, cooking, feeding family. Sustenance was canned and plastic-wrapped in every supermarket; there was little sense of real accomplishment in filling a family's bellies. She remembered chasing chickens on her father's farm, snapping the neck to cause the least pain, the proud day she plucked a chicken faster than her mother. Catching chickens, slaughtering a hog required courage, labor and a certain talent. There was a cause for pride . . .

The old room caught her glance again, and held it . . . suddenly she remembered doing things she'd never done. Trapping squirrel and rabbit, viscerating them, smoking the small strung cadavers, burying garden produce in a rock cave by the creek outside for winter storage. They were the old room's memories, not hers, and she followed them . . .

The stew pot had been simmering since dawn within the stone fireplace, the heat created in the narrow-windowed room intolerable. She stared at the blazing hearth and flinched, as though flames were sizzling against her bare arms, brown as bark. For herself, she could have lived this scorching August week on peaches, apples and raw dandelions, letting the soot-blackened hearth stand mercifully idle, cold, unlit. But a growing boy needs energy from hot cooked flesh and so she wiped the cliff of perspiration from her forehead and leaned close to stir the stew, searing her eyebrows. She stepped back quickly, slapping her face against the lingering sparks, then leaned across the open window sill for a breath of summer mountain air. The breeze filled her lungs, and it was welcome. She feared fire most of all.

Examining the pine trees beyond the window, she watched for any sudden movement of a branch, but she saw no evidence the boy was out there playing. It worried her; as she frowned, slow drops of perspiration oozed along the furrows of her brow.

The trance broke suddenly, the room was dead again, grey with cobwebs . . . Cynthia found a vacuum cleaner in the hall closet. Foolish to vacuum on such a hot morning, she told herself as she lugged the oblong machine into the kitchen. It was growing much too hot for labor, but practicality could not compete with the seductive force of the old room.

The old room shuddered, invaded by the vacuum cleaner. Its floor boards trembled under the unaccustomed suction, the windows seemed to shiver, dreading the touch of the strange machine. Cynthia vacuumed the sills and floor, the rafters and the hearth, watching dust as old as she disappear in gulps inside the hose. She sprayed cleaner on the panes, and the windows wept gratefully, blackening the mouldings. She buffed the clean glass to a shine with paper towels. Boxes and tools she stacked in one corner and when she finished, the old room gleamed and seemed to sigh as though it had miraculously survived a dreaded operation.

A *D&C*, Cynthia smiled in satisfaction. She'd scraped the womb and it was fresh to start again, building protective layers of lust and love and birth.

And, like a grateful patient who'd survived the nightmare of anesthesia, the old room trusted Cynthia, stayed with her, refused to let her go.

It was with her as she walked the manicured lawn outside and found the barely discernable dirt path that wound downhill through the tall and dry wild August grass, that led predictably and sensibly around tree trunks and glacial boulders until it spilled into the same expanse of golden flowers that she'd seen earlier from the road.

And just beyond them, as she'd envisioned earlier, stretched the creek bank.

The room was with her as she stripped off her white shorts and cotton underpants, her jersey top and pullover bra, shed her rubber sandals. Summer naked, the dark reflection of her body lay before her, rippling in the movement of the creek. She ran her hands across her shoulders, gave a shudder of freedom, and watched the reflection do the same. She placed a hand on each breast, to cover them, and the reflection, also embarrassed, timidly covered herself with her hands.

Time and space had become imperceptible, but it seemed to be the dark reflection which moved first, her toes timidly touching the creek water, concentric circles haloing her foot and ankle. The water, spring-fed, was welcome and cool. Cynthia was puzzled that she felt, at the same time, delighted and ashamed to let the water touch her nakedness.

Sinful nudity; the watchful eye of God is disapproving. Only beasts bathe as they were born, but human nakedness is displeasing to the Maker.

She heard the words in sing-song, muted voices, from the far recesses of her memory.

She had to spread her legs to hold her footing in the waist-high water. The stream had tilted the creekbed and even the mud beneath her toes was anxious to flow downhill. She clung, digging her heels and toes into the mud until they found a buried base of pebbles for traction. So entrenched, she watched the reflection of her breasts, trembling belt-like above her waist, as though she were two women, doubly endowed.

Below, creek water bathed her, entered her, darting in that soft mysterious cavern she had never seen. She placed her hand on the soft triangle and let the tiny hairs twist lovingly around her fingers, grasping as though they feared that the rapid water of the creek might sweep them from their growing place.

The sun was hot and golden on her back, she felt it loving her, and she let her fingers move in natural rhythm until the dark and shimmering shadow of her breasts peaked and her womanneed rushed downhill with the waters of the creek.

Naked, sunloved, fulfilled; then she heard the cry. The boy's shrill voice pierced the creek flow from above and flooded her with guilt.

She didn't stop for her clothes, she ran, her bare legs tearing on the tentacles of berry bushes, dry wild grass scratching her belly and her thighs, until she reached the pond, uphill, the mouth of the narrow creek.

"Pete!"

Caught in the rushing downhill water of the creek, he clung to a boulder, crying, waiting, trusting to be saved.

Angela, in a bright orange bikini, floundered near him, kicking against the current, reaching for his hand. The water was deep, Cynthia could see at a glance, and she dove

49

toward the boulder, feeling the instant chill against her heated body, then surfacing beside her frightened son.

"It's all right, darling, Mommy's here."

She was about to load the boy on her back when Angela gave a sharp strangled cry.

"Hold tight," Cynthia ordered Pete.

She reached out for Angela, flailing just downstream. Cynthia managed to pull her to the safety of the rock.

On the shore, Janet, wide-eyed, was screaming, a bizarre cheerleader at their impending tragedy.

"It's treacherous," Angela sputtered, clinging to the rock, pressing her face thankfully against the craggy boulder, "the current's strong. I didn't know or I never would have let him go out so far."

"I told you not above his head."

As though she had some way of knowing this watery terrain, Cynthia pressed both feet against the rock and pushed off, the thrust transporting her to higher ground. She stood, the water just below her breasts.

"Now," she said firmly, in a voice quite different from her own, *"hand me the boy."*

Angela held Pete with both hands firmly on his chubby waist and pushed off in the same manner, allowing Cynthia to grab him, and stretch out an arm for Angela to grasp.

Hand in hand, the women walked back toward the house, each leading a child, Cynthia acutely conscious of her nakedness, although her children had seen her body many times. Angela averted her eyes, trying not to view or admire the strong, full woman's body at her side.

"Thank you," Angela said suddenly, the tenor of her voice strange and tense. *"You trusted me with your greatest possession and I failed you."* She looked at Cynthia for only a moment before she dropped Janet's hand and ran, her head down, toward the house.

"What did she say, Mommy?" Janet's nose wrinkled as she looked up at Cynthia.

Cynthia touched her daughter's wet hair. "I don't know, dear."

"I wish I could swim more," Pete tugged reluctantly at his mother's hand.

"Mommy, next time can I go skinny-dipping too?"

"Play out here in the sun, kids," Cynthia, distracted, answered them, "and get dried off." She started for the back door, still swinging from Angela's frantic entrance. "And don't leave the yard, you hear me?"

"I'm going to take my clothes off, too," Pete's voice announced as the children seemed to fade from Cynthia's consciousness.

To follow Angela, that was the only force at work in Cynthia, to follow those long legs, that slim, straight back, that proud and trembling chin, the dark, apologetic eyes. She could not lose her.

Angela would not have gone to the old room, she had no attraction to its clutter, its quaint architecture, yet Cynhia knew she'd find her there.

Angela sat huddled, dripping, on the stone hearth, her forehead pressed against the stone facade. Cynthia knew what she'd say before she spoke and she knew, too, what the girl's responses would be; the old room gave her no choice then.

"There's no reason to weep now. The boy's safe enough."

Angela looked directly at her and Cynthia flushed with the realization of her nakedness. She turned away.

"You have too much faith in me; I don't deserve it. I only meant to help you." Angela was still crying softly.

"No harm's been done." Cynthia said doggedly, hoping that her words, repeated, would embrace the weeping girl and comfort her as she could not. *"I still trust you. You are my friend."*

"I meant to be." Angela's voice was soft and distant, a lighter tenor than her own. *"I only meant to help you, to bring you comfort."*

"And so you have." Cynthia's voice became harsh, a cloak against the deep emotion using, enveloping her.

"The boy is all you have."

"Not all."

Cynthia wanted to turn then, but she clutched her body tighter, hiding her nakedness.

"There is so much you must protect him from, so many dangers. You trusted him to me and I have failed you."

"I won't hear another word. It was God's punishment, a strike against my nakedness. I am an outrage." Cynthia left the old room as she might have stalked, angry and frustrated, from a chronic argument. She had mounted the stairs, dried and dressed, before she realized where she was and what she had been doing.

She took the steps, two at a time, down to the kitchen, clattering across the hard floor in her sandals.

Angela still sat beside the hearth.

Cynthia was about to say "I have to go back out and find my damned clothes," but before she could speak, Angela looked up and held out her arms. *"Forgive me."*

Cynthia, in the doorway, smiled awkwardly.

"Show me that you forgive me."

Cynthia moved across the old room slowly and took Angela's outstretched arms. She pulled the girl up to her feet and felt the wet and slender body press firmly against hers.

"Mommy."

Cynthia heard the screen door bang, a child's feet on the kitchen floor. She patted Angela on her bare back and smiled.

"I'll never give you reason to lose faith in me again. That is a covenant between us." Angela said.

"Yes." Cynthia held her then, feeling happy and whole.

"Mommy!"

"Trust me. We need compatriots. You and I are destined to fight this world together."

"Destined?" Cynthia laughed but felt chilled, and welcomed the continuing embrace.

"Mommy, I'm hungry!" Pete stood naked in the doorway, his baby paunch preceeding the undeveloped evidence of coming manhood.

"The sin of nakedness," Angela laughed too, still holding Cynthia close, *"I shall never understand God."*

"Hush," Cynthia replied and broke the bond between them, *"the boy has ears, you know."*

Angela gestured toward Pete's fidgeting figure in the door frame. *"He came into this world naked. Is God ashamed of his own sculpture?"*

"Hush! We'll sin too often, you and I, and we'll feel His vengeance then; mark my words."

Cynthia turned her son toward the kitchen and patted his bare behind. *"Dress yourself, son."*

"Huh?" Pete squinted, puzzled.

"Mind your mother." Angela's voice held no authority; she was amused.

Pete didn't budge.

"He won't be fit for life without some discipline."

Cynthia smacked Pete's bare behind. He hollered, in shocked protest.

"Don't beat him for what's natural. You mustn't be as they are."

"He must learn to obey, or he'll be as damned as I am. God's punishment is strict and harsh."

"Martha?"

Cynthia turned with no surprise; she was responding to her name.

"Martha, according to the book, God is love."

"Mommy, I'm hungry. Did you get the Wheaties?" Janet burst, naked, through the screen door, tossing Pete's frisbee between her hands.

"That's mine, gimme!"

When she stepped into the kitchen to separate her squalling children, Cynthia became herself again.

She'd poured milk on the Wheaties, and wiped up two spills, before Angela came out of the old room, slowly, dazed, as though awakening from a long, deep sleep.

They didn't speak of it, not all the hot length of the afternoon. The children, too, sensed something not quite explainable and asked no questions of the adults.

Playing Olympics in the back yard, Pete broad-jumped the narrow rock path, rolled in the dirt and sat up grinning, clover in his hair.

"How come they talk so funny?"

"You cheated," his sister answered, hands on hips, "you stepped on the path to push off."

"Didn't."

"Did!"

"How come they talk so funny?"

"That jump doesn't count. You'll have to do it over."

"Who died and made you boss?" He'd heard his father say that to his mother.

"I'm the official, I'll disqualify you."

Pete crossed the path and got his pudgy body into position to make the jump again. He paused and turned to his sister. "How did you get to be official?"

"I'm biggest," she said factually. "The biggest people are always in charge."

Pete jumped again and landed, splat, on his plump belly, his pudgy face immersed in sunbrowned grass.

His sister laughed, and when she did, nothing in the world could make him cry.

Angela slept on the sunporch, feverish in the window-filtered sun. Through sporadic dreams, she heard the children's voices and fell into a wafting memory of her lonely girlhood. Motherless, her father a man's man with good intentions but lacking the ability to nurture, she'd looked for love in neighbor women, cradling her head in strange bosoms, hungry for a mother's soft kiss.

"I'll kill the boy who touches you," her father had vowed, crazy with concern about the daughter he was forced to bring up without a mother. There was no reason for such protectiveness at the time he said it; Angela was then a scrawny, leggy girl whose baby teeth went late and who suffered adolescent skin too early. By the time she'd blossomed, duckling into swan, and boys showed interest, she shied away. Men puzzled her just as her father puzzled her. They frightened her, just as her father did.

Angela had had crushes on teachers and neighbors before she left her father's house, before she felt that she could call herself a woman. The feeling that she had for Cynthia was the strongest, though, perhaps because she lived alone now, free of her father's watchful eye, and the possibility existed that her fantasy might seep into reality. The possibility was remote, and Angela was clearly, painfully aware of that fact. She could not reach out or make her needs known, she was far too shy and much too terrified to chance rejection. Unspoken love was safest.

She welcomed the possession of the old room. It was a guise to bring her close to Cynthia with no fear of recrimination. They were caught in something stronger than themselves; Angela was grateful to feel the old room seize her hidden feelings, dredge them from their protected place inside her, and cast them wildly into the clean, gold air of sunlight.

She couldn't speak of it. She was afraid that if she spoke of it, she would break the spell. She could not see clearly yet what lay beyond this woman-woman closeness, but Angela knew that she would flow with it, wherever it might lead. She turned, her body damp with perspiration, on the cot beneath the sunfilled window, feeling the heat change focus, spread warmth across her back. She dreamed of Cynthia as they'd driven the long road to Massachusetts, Cynthia behind the steering wheel, wisps of blonde hair fluttering above her forehead and her temples, turning to the left or to the right, accelerating, braking, in control, confidently delivering them to their destination. Angela would follow Cynthia and the old room.

Cynthia sat at the kitchen table, sorting her art supplies, blowing dust from paint tube caps and from the aged, yellowed canvas. When the sun sunk westward, she would outfit the old room, set up her studio, but now the afternoon heat hung heavy over her and she was tired, depleted and confused.

She'd been bred strong. Her mother saw to that. An alcoholic farmer can't tend crops, see over personnel, keep books. A man daily hungover, listless, cannot give love, support to an eager, growing daughter. The women ran the farm and attributed its middling success to him, assumed responsibility for its failures. They joined their limbs like slender birch, clumping for mutual support, and gave him credit for the family unity.

It was the memory of her father, long and lean, short-tempered and prone to violent though brief explosions, that led Cynthia to Dave. Plump and gentle, calm and steady, Dave was the opposite of everything that she despised in men. And yet he needed her, just as her father had. Without her, Dave would not have gambled on his own business, would not have formed the block association or joined the civilian street patrol; without her, he was wise and kind and tender. Cynthia was his staff of courage, and his excuse, if and when he failed.

She loved him because he needed her. He loved her because she needed him to need her. They meshed like gears in complicated machinery, spinning interlocked in perfect tandem. Should one gear speed up or slow down, the system failed. Their marriage tolerated little change.

She wrote a note there on the kitchen table, her script across the paper as open and loving as her feelings. "Arrived safe, kids think the place's terrific. So do I. Love you." She put the pen down, then lifted it again and added, "Miss you," although she didn't. She gasped for such moments of freedom and, from a distance, love was pure, it didn't burp or frown or grump. She licked a stamp and wondered if the temperamental New York City mails would deliver the note before Dave left to join them. He was arriving Friday. A few days, that's all she had without him; she felt a strong, sharp sense of panic.

Something was happening to her in this house, something so powerful she couldn't speak of it. She ought to say, "What the hell is happening here?" She ought to stay out of the old room. But all the *oughts* could not contain her now, she was beyond them, too far into an adventure to turn back. She felt excitement, certainly, and foreboding. It would be cowardly to turn tail; the old room needed her. She needed it, she needed an experience of magnitude, a secret Dave could never share. If she spoke of it, the children or Angela might repeat her words to Dave. "What do you mean?" he'd say. "You mean you saw a ghost? I had an aunt once who had a spirit in her closet, used to knock the hangers off the rod. . . ." It was too precious, this thing that was surrounding her, she would not let its secret, or her own, be violated, bantered, shared. She looked at the old room, squatting and leaning against the main house, its timbers heavy, simmering in the August sun. Like a small child, she pursed her lips and pressed her upright finger to them. *Shhhh* . . . she said aloud.

56

Pete, who'd refused to succumb to his usual nap after lunch, was sleeping soundly in the canvas hammock on the porch.

Janet sat on the front steps, playing a half-hearted game of jacks. She felt left out. She often felt left out. Most of her playtime hung heavy with the responsibility of little Pete, and schooldays she was charged with being super-student, to maintain the scholarship that kept her in a private elementary school. Cynthia assumed that her daughter would mature early, readily accept the burden of a little brother, of helping with the laundry, of cooking for the family when her mother was away. Cynthia herself had run a household at Janet's age, when her mother was busy with the business of the family farm. Little girls have little time for childhood; their pranks are considered peevish. Protectiveness and nurturing are stirred in them early, they are set adrift too soon, and protesting, small girls whine.

Janet was whining silently now inside herself, jealous of her brother, hungry for attention. The feeling that she didn't belong gnawed at her. She had no friends on this hillside, no one who loved her most, the best of all. Pete and her father received most of her mother's attentions when they were home. They needed it, Cynthia said. Angela ran ragged taking care of Pete and, sometimes, of both her parents, but nobody centered attention solely on Janet.

"She's such a good girl, so well behaved, we never have to worry about Janet, she'll take care of herself."

At noon, in the kitchen, when her mother and Angela had embraced and talked so strangely, Janet felt as though they hadn't seen her, didn't know she still existed. They'd gone into another world, Pete with them, deserting and denying her. As Janet had rubbed her signature off a drawing that was not quite good enough, scrubbing the rough paper raw with a hard red eraser, so her mother and Angela had erased her from their strange, new world.

They had taken Pete, though, and Janet hated him for that. Watching him sleep, cherubic and roly-poly in the hammock, Janet wished her little brother dead.

She scooped up all her jacks and stuffed them, with the

small black ball, into the pocket of her shorts. She didn't ask permission—nobody cared anyway—and she walked with strong defiant steps down the rutted dirt road toward the bottom of the hill, hoping she would find a friend there.

Chapter Five

Red Richmond knew next to nothing about small girls. He knew boys, he'd been one himself, but he'd had no sisters or girl playmates, and secretly he considered young females cantankerous. They cried, he thought, and whined and moaned and marked time quite unattractively until they blossomed into womanhood.

He saw Janet approaching his back screen door. "It's too hot for riding today," he called, hoping she'd turn tail and return to her mother's proper custody. "Horses overheat the same as cars."

But she kept coming, smiling, looking hopeful. Red had a flash of memory, of undated girls who stood along the sidelines at a dance, begging for attention with their bovine eyes.

He sighed and watched the child pull back the screen door, step inside the old log cabin that his father built.

"Hello." Her voice, high and girlish, was assertive.

"Hi there." Red donned his most fake genial manner, unaware that children can see through facades.

He didn't like her, either, Janet knew that right away; he wished she'd leave, evaporate. He turned back to the paper he was reading and cut her out, as Angela and her mother had done earlier.

If I have something that he wants, he'll like me.

Janet didn't think those words, she had no words for treachery as yet, but the impulse was quite natural, a by-product of her survival instinct. She didn't understand the ties between men and women, either, but she knew the lie that would spark interest in Red Richmond.

"Angela's my best friend."

"Oh?" Red Richmond smiled; no little boy would claim

a babysitter as a best friend. A babysitter, bound by duty to retard adventure, exploration, was more warden than friend to any natural born male. His respect for the girl dropped another notch.

"She's taking a nap now."

Red nodded, trying to concentrate on baseball scores and wishing that the girl would go away.

"I expect she'll be real lonely when my daddy gets here. She won't have Mommy to talk to every night."

Janet felt an old jealousy simmer in her belly. Daddy and Mommy, Mommy and Angela, grownups whispering and sharing grownup secrets while she lay still in her bed, straining to hear, feeling so alone she feared she'd disappear if she allowed sleep to overtake her. She always bundled herself in quilts, no matter how hot the weather, as a precaution against invisibility.

"Oh?" Red's voice showed interest.

"I go up to her apartment in New York practically all the time." Another lie.

"Is that so?" Red folded the paper, face down, across his lap.

"She lives all by herself and hasn't any husband. She gets real lonely." Janet waited for a response. "She tells me lots of things."

"Like what?" He lit a cigarette and motioned for Janet to sit down.

She conjured up her most mysterious voice. "Secret."

"Girl talk, huh?" Red nodded, laughed. He paused, and tried to ask casually, "She got a boyfriend?"

Janet pursed her lips. In fact, she'd never seen a boyfriend, but all girls had boyfriends, she knew that. Even she called stupid Bobby Blair her boyfriend.

"I can't tell, it's a secret."

"Come on," Red said, as though he didn't give a damn, but Janet knew.

"Well . . . . Promise not to tell I told you?"

"Cross my heart."

"Promise to take me riding on a horse?"

"I swear it."

"And swimming in the creek, too? Mommy won't let me go alone."

"Hey, hey, wait a minute." Red laughed self-consciously. "I've only got so much time, you know."

Janet knew he had the summer free, she could smell it; no odor of anxiety or pressure. There was a different smell about her daddy on the weekends than on weekdays, and she could smell that Red Richmond was a weekend man all week.

"If I tell, I might lose my best friend, then I'd need another, wouldn't I?"

"You drive some bargain, kid." Red added *devious* to his list of adjectives applying to small girls.

"Will you be my friend?"

Red shrugged. "Yeah. Does she have a boyfriend?"

Janet grinned; she'd won. She shook her head verociously. "Nope."

Red smiled and leaned back, reconstructing Angela in his mind. Lean but well-proportioned, the kind of girl you could take to a relative's for dinner, the kind of girl you could write poems to, hold hands along the creekbank with, a girl to take to bed at night, warm belly under his, eager thighs wrapped round his waist, urging the hard length of him inside her, sucking him home again inside a womb.

"Come on, friend," he said to Janet, and rose from the chair, "I'll walk you home."

The rabbit was full-grown, muscular and wise. The fox was small and boney, still young enough for suckling. It caught the rabbit with its first lunge, almost by accident, springing across the roadway, drilling its baby teeth into the rabbit's back. The hare kicked hard and spun the young fox backward. It landed on its shoulders, stunned. The hare limped for the safety of the brush beside the road. The fox rolled over, crouched; Red and Janet saw its eyes, wild and determined. It leapt three times its length, a red flash, to tear the rabbit's throat from ear to long ear. The rabbit kicked feebly once then lay, lifeless, at the fox's feet. The fox sprawled beside its victim, as though in grief for an old friend. Gently it grasped the open wound and pulled, ripping free a pink and still shiny piece of flesh.

Janet stared, fascinated, transfixed. Another piece of

flesh, long and thick veined, blood spurting, matted the full, dead rabbit's hair.

"That fox," Red said softly, awed "is much too small to be out on his own. That's why he's so damned fast and vicious. He's got to be in order to survive."

Janet didn't hear him. She only heard the savage ripping of the rabbit's carcass, continued to stare at the mass of veins and mucus in the open flank, and wondered if Pete looked like that inside his skin.

Red shuddered and took the girl's hand, as much for his comfort as for hers. He stepped forward to lead her past, and the fox snarled, spat and backed into the brush, warning them to bypass his dinner.

Angela felt as though she'd been asleep for days, for months, for centuries. She had no notion where she was when Red tapped on the window by her head.

"Good afternoon."

Bearded like the devil. She didn't recognize him; her half-sleep thoughts made no sense. Devils had beards.

She sat up and shook her head.

Red looked around for his young escort before he climbed the steps and opened the door to the sunporch, but Janet had darted out of sight.

She was heading for the kitchen, hoping to reclaim her mother. "Mommy?"

Cynthia was in the old room, sitting in the sapling chair, smiling, staring out the window to the pines beyond.

"Mommy?"

Janet stood in the doorframe; she knew she wasn't being heard. Outside the narrow window of the old room, she could see her brother playing in the pine cones, a direct line between his bustling body and her mother's watchful eye.

"Mommy? I went to the bottom of the hill all by myself." Cynthia didn't hear. Janet opened the refrigerator in the kitchen noisily, took out a cold carton of white milk and poured a puddle on the floor. Her mother didn't turn, didn't look at her. She slammed the refrigerator door so hard that the entire machine rocked, banging against the wall.

Cynthia continued to smile at Pete.

Janet ran furiously, tracking white footprints of milk, down the hall, up the stairway and into her own room. She wrapped the quilt around her shoulders.

They mustn't find him, Cynthia was thinking, *they mustn't know the boy is alive. They'll be bound to take him and he'll have a wretched life with them. He'll be as marked as I am. Only God can judge us, here.*

A yellow dog, its thick coat burred, darted from the stand of pines and approached Pete warily, sniffing in a circle around the boy's bare feet.

"Mother," Pete called, a strange new expression on his face, *Mother, I believe we've found a friend."*

"I believe it's he who's done the finding. Be careful if you touch him, son; he may have been mistreated."

Pete squatted and held out his small hand, palm down, patient until the dog had sniffed, was satisfied and licked his fingers. He hugged the dog's thick neck then and pressed his cheek against the dog's wet muzzle.

Cynthia smiled. *The boy needs a creature of his own to cherish. A boy needs a friend. And I,* she mused, *I also need a friend, but a yellow dog won't do for me.*

She remembered the long death of her mother, hacking, lungs snarled, unable to find breath, curled like the unborn, winterbound before the hearth. The long walk to the village in snow high enough to freeze her homespun skirts had done no good. It only served to remind the townsfolk that a fallen woman, driven from the village, lived on a lonely hill with her daughter. And if God wanted to take the woman, He would find no interference from the villagers. They knew the girl could hardly last the winter by herself but her death by freezing or starvation wasn't their concern. Their thoughts were pure; God's will would be done.

But she had survived the winter, after burying her mother's wretched corpse beneath the drifts, until spring thawed the ground. And she'd survived the summer and the following winter and yet another year, and then another, until the town forgot about the cabin on the hill and its ill-fated oc-cupant.

He'd found her, though, in early spring, hauling his ped-dler's cart from town to town. He'd seen her swimming na-ked in the creek, across the yellow field of flowers, and he'd spoken gently to her and given her a new iron cooking pot, a sharpened ax head and a pair of carders. She had no sheep, but rabbit hair had made a blanket and a cloak.

The act itself had not felt good, it pierced and hurt her and she bled then as she bled on the rise of each quarter moon. It was not the act itself that she remembered with such powerful joy, it was the nearness and the touching, his hair across her forehead, his fingers stroking the long line of her throat.

She needed the iron pot, the ax head and the carders, but the gratefulness that still rose in her throat was not for those gifts from his jingling cart. She loved him, she sup-posed, for caring for one sunlit afternoon, for touching her and talking, for listening and leaving her belly full with living memory.

The boy was born easily that winter; she gave birth to him the way she'd seen wild dogs bear pups. She couldn't let the village know that he'd been born here, bastard of a bastard, and they lived together quietly, boy and woman, learning to silence squeals of pleasure, shouts of joy, forcing the land to feed them, filling the tiny cabin with love for each other and a strong, unspoken yearning for human freedom.

It's hard talking to the boy sometimes, Cynthia thought as she sat in the worn sapling chair, *hard telling him the things that lie inside a woman. She longed for the vanished peddler, for her dead mother, for a lover, for a friend, and her longing filled the little room.*

"I've done most everything I wanted," Red was saying to Angela; he sat beside her in the lounge chair, "bummed Europe, lived in a commune, weathered a winter in a shack on Cape Cod, I've had enough adventure. I'm ready to set-tle down."

He grinned, blushed and glanced at her from the corner of his eye. She shook her head; although she was awake now, she couldn't shake the lingering, subsurface life within her.

"My folks would like to see me settle on the hill; that's why I've been thinking about buying this old house."

Angela smiled politely, weakly, and felt peculiarly threatened.

"Dad built our cabin with his own two hands, but the land's been in his family forever."

Angela nodded and looked through the window, trying to catch a glimpse of either child, feeling trapped against Red's body in the lounge chair.

"They'd sure love it if I settled down in this old house." Red patted the bannister with such familiar fervor that Angela reacted as though his hand had taken possession of her thigh. "They'd be in spoiling distance of their grandchildren."

Angela moved as far from Red as the chair arm would allow and called out the window, "Janet!"

"I think I saw her go upstairs . . . I've got a teaching license, if there're ever any openings in the village school. I'm also pretty handy with my hands; I might become a plumber. The village plumber's seventy, he can't hold out much longer." Red laughed and looked at Angela, expecting appreciation.

She smiled distantly, tilting her body away from his. "Pete!"

"He was playing in the yard when we came in, I saw him. He can't go far, he's just a kid."

"I'd better look for him," Angela insisted, standing up suddenly, straightening her sleep-rumpled clothes, "I'm responsible for him."

Red rose reluctantly and held the porch door open for her.

"You'll make a damned good mother someday."

Angela half-nodded, and walked swiftly to the corner of the house.

"Listen, I'll drop in again tomorrow, okay?"

Angela waved and started for the back yard.

"Feel free to come down to my place, too. Any time."

But Angela had disappeared.

Red shrugged, shoved his hands deep into his pockets and ambled down the rutted dirt road toward his cabin.

She saw him for the first time, a young blond boy rolling in pine needles with a yellow dog. She stopped and smiled. She'd never walked so far up in these woods before, not even with her father when he'd dressed her up in boy's breeches and taken her to hunt squirrel.

"I haven't got a boy," he'd said to her, "and so you'll have to be one," but when he died and left her in the shack beside the main road, with no property, no goods, the sole survivor of a tenant farmer, she'd let her hair grow and worn the long skirts that her mother'd brought in trunks from Lancashire. Her mother had been a lady, she remembered, and remembered, too, the words she'd learned to spell and write under her mother's tutelage. Her mother hadn't taken well to travel, and disliked the colonies. It was with anger that her father had allowed book learning. "Better," he'd said, "that both you women learn to build and farm in this new land."

And then one day, just as the girl was learning to script numbers, her mother left. "She's gone home." That was all her father would say about the disappearance; the girl never knew whether her mother had sailed safely back to England or if she hovered somewhere above her head, joyous in a final heavenly home.

It was well she'd learned to hunt squirrel and to grow squash. At her father's death, she was wholly dependent on her own devices. A young man from the village once saw her from the road and came to pay court, but she had no dowry, and no interest in him . . . She couldn't farm the landlord's land, however; that had become her current challenge. The Richmonds wanted a family on the land, maintaining the house, cultivating the forested acres of land for profit.

The youngest Richmond had an eye for her, she saw that, and it was purely by the grace of this attraction that they hadn't yet evicted her. Sooner or later, she thought, he'd call for payment, but until then she could walk the wooded hill and try to think of pleasant things, a future for herself.

66

She'd never known that a boy lived on this hilltop although she'd heard from peddlers that a fallen woman had died in a hidden cabin at the peak.

The boy stopped rolling with the dog when he first caught a glimpse of her and held the mongrel's neck tight, frozen, frightened.

"Good afternoon," she said gently, softly. "You may speak to me, you know. I haven't come to harm you."

The boy glanced at the window of the cabin, at his mother who sat sternly, stiff-backed behind the glass.

Cynthia's heart froze when she saw the dark young woman. *A lady, one could tell from her dress, an official's wife or daughter lost on the hillside, running mischeviously or angrily from her father or husband. Whichever, he'd come looking for her and the boy would be seized. Fallen women and their bastards were considered dangerous, corruptors of good men.*

Hot, angry tears filled Cynthia's eyes. *God was everywhere. Why had she thought that she could hide from Him? He promised judgment. Here it was, in long-haired form, with warm and sparkling eyes, an avenging angel.*

"Good afternoon!" The dark girl's voice was musical. She peeked inside the cabin, raping it with curious eyes.

Cynthia's body went rigid. *No one had ever seen this cabin but her father, mother, her son and herself. It was their family hiding place, the guilty gift of her father, whose name she did not know for certain, whose name her mother never spoke except to say he was a married man, a land owner, and eager to free-lease this useless hilltop to his mistress, as assurance that she wouldn't return to the village with her bastard child, and point a finger his way.*

Her faceless father had built this cabin by moonlight, sawing in thunder storms so that no sound would reverberate, alert the villagers. He commanded high respect in the village, her mother said, and she knew he must have a streak of decency within him because he had built a home and given them land, if not his name.

When she had walked to town, on the eve of her mother's death, a small girl in frozen homespun, begging for help, she'd studied the faces of the gentlemen, and when a

*man with eyes as navy blue as her own touched her shoul-
der gently, before he sent her back, unaided, to die beside
her mother on the hill, she'd thought he was her father.
She'd tried, in the intervening years, to keep his face in
front of her but she'd lost his features, one by one, until the
man she believed to be her father was a blur in ruffled shirt
and brown vest and breeches. She lost his face, but she
would never lose his name: the Elder Richmond.*

"I haven't come to harm you," the young woman repeated, to Cynthia.

Cynthia sat stiffly, unable to utter a sound.

"I suppose you don't have many visitors up here." The
*young woman leaned across the open window sill, smiling.
"I didn't know that anybody lived up here. I thought this
hill was Richmond land."*

Cynthia nodded, forced herself to speak, *"By law, it is."*

"I live on Richmond land myself," the young woman
*smiled again, "the tenant farm on the main road. I'm
afraid,"* she added cheerfully, *"I shall be homeless soon.
My father died, and no one's left to farm the land. The
Elder Richmond places a limit on his charity."*

Cynthia smiled and relaxed slightly; she still felt cau-
tious, but the terror that had frozen her was gone.

"I'm known as Abigail," the dark young woman said.

"My mother, God rest her soul, called me Martha."

"And the boy?"

"Jeremiah." It was the peddler's name.

"He gets no schooling up here?"

"He doesn't need it."

"He might go to the village someday."

"Never."

*"My mother taught me reading, writing and some num-
bering before she went away."*

"My mother taught me reading but no numbers."

*"I could teach you and Jeremiah, if that would please
you."*

"We don't take charity."

"For trade, then. A bed and food in trade for learning."

"I've only got one bed. The boy sleeps on a pallet."

"I could share the boy's pallet."

Martha flushed and stiffened, imagining the temptations of the dark young woman in bed with a growing boy.

"No. If you wish to stay here, you'll share the bed with me."

Abigail smiled broadly. "I wish to stay."

"But you must swear that when you leave this hill, you'll tell no one you know me, the boy or this cabin."

Abigail nodded.

"Swear it."

"I swear."

"Come inside, friend." "Martha stood, then walked to the cabin door.

Janet crept downstairs, the quilt still wrapped around her shoulders. Surely someone would have missed her by this time. She pattered barefoot into the kitchen; her mother was standing at the doorway to the old room, smiling warmly, welcome on her face.

"I spilt some milk." Janet said softly, her words thickly padded with fear and guilt, but her mother continued smiling distantly. Janet got a dishtowel and squatted to mop up, glancing nervously, between swipes, at her mother's constant smile. When Janet had wrung out the dishcloth, and all evidence of her tantrum was gone, she spoke quite loudly, need overcoming the nervous tremble in her stomach.

"Mommy, will you play *Scrabble* with me before supper?"

Cynthia heard words, but they were far away and indistinguishable.

"You promised we'd play *Scrabble* every night when we got up here."

A moment, and the past whined into silence, a record player losing power. Cynthia's eyes, still warm, focused on her daughter.

"Get the board, honey, and set it up. Let's play on the porch and watch the sun set."

Janet's heart quickened and she dropped the quilt, a patchwork pile in the center of the kitchen floor. She ran upstairs to fetch the *Scrabble* board. It was the best game, because Pete couldn't spell and couldn't play.

Cynthia poured a glass of milk for Janet, some white wine for herself. She sauntered toward the front porch; she had never felt so breathlessly elated, not at her marriage, not at her children's births, never the high, taunting melody inside her that she felt this night. Something beautiful was going to happen and her heart was open to it.

Angela was bouyant. She and Pete were playing jacks on the porch floor beside Cynthia and Janet. Pete, whose small hand had difficulty encompassing the ball, suddenly accused Angela of cheating.

"Because you don't win, does not mean that the other person's cheating." Cynthia reprimanded him, to Janet's pleasure.

"I want to win!"

Cynthia grinned at her small son and shook her head. "Everybody wants to win, but in every contest there can only be one winner."

The yellow dog whined at the screen door.

"Why can't he come in, Mommy?"

"I don't want you to get too attached to him, Pete. He belongs to somebody, I'm sure. Besides, we can't take him home with us."

Pete pressed his nose against the screen. "He's hungry."

Cynthia sighed. "Feed him. But keep him outside. I'm sure he's full of fleas and ticks."

"Come on, Angela," Pete said; he tugged at her hand, pulling her toward the kitchen, "let's get some supper for him. There, boy, go to the kitchen door."

The dog tucked its tail between its legs, slinking around the corner of the house.

"I'd rather have a cat," Janet said.

"Cats shed," her mother replied, placing three blocks on the *Scrabble* board.

LOVE.

"I've got one!" Janet spread five blocks across the board. Then her face fell. "It's a proper name, I can't use it."

VICTOR.

"It's a word, too," her mother said, "it means winner."

"Really?" Janet beamed; she only had one letter left.

Cynthia added two letters in front of MAN.

WOMAN.

Janet smiled slyly, took her last letter and placed it in front of AD.

DAD.

"I win!"

Cynthia smiled at her. "I'm glad."

Cynthia sipped her wine and watched Janet carefully and neatly replace the letters in the box. Cynthia tried to remember being seven and a half, but it seemed somehow she was the same age—whether it was five and a half, seven and a half or ten and a half—until the year she was sixteen, old enough to call herself a woman. A girl was pleasant, she thought: they reared themselves, assumed responsibility; reflection of herself, small parcel of immortality.

A boy, on the other hand, required constant attention. He was more likely to fall from a tree, run into a road after a stray dog, break a leg on a bike, get slashed in a fight. A boy didn't often stop to look where he was going; a mother had to be his eyes, his leash, his conscience.

She was thankful that she'd had her girl first, compatriot in mothering.

"How many days 'til Daddy comes?" Janet folded the board carefully into the box.

"Three more, darling. He'll be here Friday."

"I miss him." Janet said factually, without a whine. Sometimes her father held her, lifted her, swung her around, gave her moments of childhood freedom.

"I miss him, too."

At that moment, for that moment, Cynthia did miss him. She remembered his warm naked back in bed. She always slept against it, her arm thrown around his plump waist, her cheek pressed hard enough against his shoulder blades that she could hear the steady beating of his heart.

She wondered if he'd done a laundry this week, or if he'd arrive on Friday with a suitcase full of neatly folded dirty shirts and soiled underwear. She hoped at least he'd wash the dishes Thursday night, not leave them soaking in a soapy sink, curdling the water with congealing grease. When he cooked, he did so with bravado, flourish, and dirtied nearly every pot and pan in the process. He'd wash a plate or cup and smile; he'd done his share, leaving the silverware and greasy pans sitting mid-sink "They need to soak, I'll do them later." Once she had left them for eleven days, washing the daily dishes around and over them, before she heaved a despairing sigh and plunged a brillo pad into the standing water. She hoped he'd closed the deal with *Continental Coffees,* that the commission on the job would be enough to float his business for a while. "I could be on a salary," he'd say, each time he sat down to pay bills. The statement was directed at her and she knew it. If he succeeded, he'd graciously give credit to her, "Cynthia talked me into doing it," but if he failed, she'd be blamed.

Dave would crumple a fender; it would be the other guy's fault. He'd spill an icetray; the children had distracted him and made him do it. He'd gain five pounds so that his shirt wouldn't button; it was the manufacturer's fault for making clothes that shrank. He'd had a girlfriend, before he married, a glamorous, seductive, big spender who wound him around her finger. "I'd have some money now if I hadn't spent it all on Gloria," he still said, every time the rent fell due, "she really took me." Cynthia shuddered at the anger he'd harbor toward her should his business fail.

He was a paradox, her roly-poly husband. Affectionate and giving as long as his gifts brought success (the money he'd spent on Gloria failed to keep her; she'd left him for a Miami beach bum when Dave had paid the tab to take her south for a vacation), he could not tolerate failure in a world where things and people fail more often than they succeed. No appliance made satisfied him. The toaster hummed, the TV set was not crystal clear as it had been in the display window before they bought it, the movie projector broke down one day past its warranty. Each time he used an appliance he muttered loudly about its inefficiency and Cynthia shuddered inwardly; since it was generally her responsibility to purchase such appliances, he seemed to be blaming her for the buzz she couldn't hear, the rattle she would never have noticed. She dreaded the purchasing of anything for the household, it was sure to displease Dave, and returning things, time and again to hostile shopkeepers sent shivers of resentment through her.

"Lady, they all buzz like this. That's the way they make them. You can't hardly hear it. It works fine, don't it?"

The fact was, she couldn't hear the buzz at all. "My husband wants the buzz taken out of it."

"I'll give you a new one, lady, but it's gonna sound the same way."

"Well, did you ask him?" Dave would say when she returned, her innards trembling, "Did you ask him why they make them that way? Did you tell him that you won't accept a toaster with a buzz in it?"

"Take it yourself next time!" But if he did, she'd feel guilty because he really hadn't time to hassle with it, and he'd return home, just as she did, with no satisfaction and a rage that lasted several hours.

He remembered, like an elephant, the purchase date and price of everything in the apartment, but he never knew where things were. "Where're the knives, honey?" "Where'd you put my shirts?" "Where's the afternoon paper?" The knives and shirts and paper were always in the same place, year after year, yet he always asked and waited until Cynthia fetched the items for him. It seemed to please him when she left what she was doing and, struggling not to show her irritation, handed him the knife or shirt or paper that was already within his reach. It was his way, she thought, of guaranteeing that she'd pay attention to him, as though he lived in constant fear of being excluded from her life.

She knew he didn't like her to paint. The very act of painting shut him out. This was a good excuse for her to avoid painting; it was selfish, instilled guilt. She could say that it was his fault she no longer painted. Their marriage was ingrown, they fed on one another's weaknesses, dependencies. They gobbled one another up and got bloated with a sense of security, knowing each one depended on the other for survival.

Snuggled in the darkness, his teddy bear body enveloping her, he'd speak softly, frightened as a child.

"I know you're going to leave me. Some other guy's going to come along . . . . "

He saved frightened kittens from trees in Central Park, and carried old ladies' grocery bags from the supermarket.

73

He gave of his time (and sometimes hers) to anyone who needed him. He loved people in a way she did not (his passion for people as great as his antipathy for appliances), and was genuinely concerned about such things as the health of Mrs. Santimeyer's cat on the third floor. Cynthia had no interest in Mrs. Santimeyer or her cat but she felt she had to remember to inquire about both each day, knowing that would be one of the myriad of questions Dave would ask when he came through the door each night.

He had no need for privacy at all and was happiest when friends and neighbors dropped in and out of the apartment with no warning. Sharing an experience with Dave was to lose it for herself. Social and effervescent, he pounced on each experience, devoured it, retold it to their friends so well embroidered with his point of view that Cynthia lost the meaning of it for herself.

He would invade the old room when he came. He'd sense its importance to her right away, he had a knack for that. He'd bustle busily about the floor boards, rapping rafters, pushing himself between her and the old room.

"Have you asked about this room in town, have you gone to town hall, there must be records somewhere, have you described the structure to a carpenter? A carpenter could tell the age right off. Have you said to anybody in town, 'We have this old one room cabin attached to the Rogers' house, and it looks as though it pre-dates the Revolution; do you know anything about it?' Have you asked that?"

He'd attack her with his questions until the old room became his as much as hers.

Cynthia stood up suddenly and followed Janet to the kitchen. She stared at the worn door frame to the old room and smiled the fierce, protective smile of threatened woman.

Chapter Six

It was still light after they ate supper, washed dishes, watched a sleepy raccoon hesitantly discover and explore the garbage cans. The children were weary early, snapping and whining, and Angela shuffled them upstairs for baths and bed.

There was no light in the old room, no rubbercoated cable to extend electricity within the worn walls. Cynthia sat in the slowly fading dusk and arranged her paints along the wooden shelf built into the wall. The sapling chair was comfortable beneath her, its ancient caning sprung just right as though accustomed to her very haunches. Three boxes stacked against the rough sawn headboard of the old bed served as a makeshift easel, and she placed the canvas on them, staring, conjuring a picture.

She'd always liked painting landscapes, barns crumbling in a field of weeds, stalwart farmhouses standing stiffbacked in a changing, world. Her acceptance at art school had been based on a painting of the long unused privy behind her father's barn.

She knew what she would paint then, what she would bring to life on this gray, dusty canvas. The corner of the old room, the stone fireplace, the old wood walls, sagging, weary with the relentless burden of passing time. In the corner of the splintered window frame, she'd paint a spider web, its occupant the only living creature in this forgotten room. She smiled and took the piece of charcoal in her fingers, broke it to rough surface and began, despite the growing dimness, to sketch the outline of the painting she'd created in her mind.

An hour later, when Angela appeared in the doorway, Cynthia was sketching still, although the last usable rays of daylight were long gone.

"I don't know how you can see what you're doing."

It wasn't Cynthia who turned and smiled, held out her hand.

"The boy's asleep?"

Abigail nodded.

"You're good to him. I appreciate that."

"Tomorrow, I will fetch my things from Richmond's house. I haven't much—my mother's dishes, my father's hoe, his rake and ax."

"I've only two plates and two bowls here; we'll make use of the dishes. We'll need the tools, with two of us to garden, too. I'll go with you, to help you carry."

"You might be seen. The main road's used by farmers now as well as peddlers."

"What can they do to me but hurl their insults?"

"And their stones. They'd chase you, just for sport, and they might find the boy. They'd take him away from you, you know that."

"We'll go tonight then."

The downhill road was dark. No light glowed even in the Richmond cabin, nestled at the foot.

Hand in hand, the women walked, their fingers comfort to each other, smiling in the darkness at the sense they both had of a new beginning.

Abigail, with ears like deer, heard it first. She stopped motionless and listened, then pulled Martha into the brush beside her, out of sight.

They rode, six horsemen, holding their torches high, crying out *"God's will be done!"* Lashed to a cart behind the final rider, two women screamed in terror.

Martha's heart beat wildly, pounding against her ribcage. The moonlight struck the cart and she saw the horror stricken faces of the women, their eyes wide, their mouths dropped in terror, emitting constant piercing screams, as the motion of the cart flailed their lashed bodies one against the other.

"Witches." Abigail whispered. *"They'll be burned to-night."*

Martha gasped and started. Her instinct was to run, a wild creature tearing through the bramble, but Abigail held her hand.

"The road will fill up now," Abigail predicted. *"Farmers and peddlers will ride to town to see the burning. We dare not cross the road tonight."*

Abigail moved swiftly to a sheltered clearing and sat down in the shadow of an oak. *"We'll wait here. It would be foolhardy to move about until the thing is done."*

Martha sat quietly beside her new friend. Her knees were trembling, and she wrapped her arms about them.

"What have they done, the women, to displease God?" She asked so softly that Abigail leaned forward in the dark to catch her words.

"In mid-winter, a peddler's woman was burned for her loose conduct. I saw the peddler after; he stopped for water. He said that there are witches everywhere and man must learn to recognize them or he'll lose his soul. He said he would have never known his woman was a witch. The Elders recognized it right away, he said."

"How can they tell, the Elders?" Martha pressed her back against the sturdy tree as though she had the power to part its bark, to hide herself within its trunk.

"In spring, they burned the midwife from the bay. She'd been possessed, they said, and gave delivery to a boy with one eye and a forked tail."

Martha gasped.

Her milk was sour, too, they said, and nearly poisoned three infants . . . They tried to burn the Granny on the North Road, too, for poisoning good men with her herbs and leeches. She doctored Elder Samson's boy when he got thrown, breaking in his horse, and he died in seven days. When the Granny heard that they'd set out to burn her, she dove into the bay and disappeared. Witches can do that, so they say."

Martha closed her eyes and took long, deep breaths, hoping to slow the frantic beating of her heart.

"They have no shame, witches. They bare their breasts and tempt men to lose their souls. They say that you can

tell a witch by smelling her fingertips; she's sure to have placed her hands inside the parts of her that are condemned by God."

Martha remembered the cool mornings she'd spent naked in the creek, her fingers bringing the forbidden pleasure. Like Eve, she had succumbed to the wily serpent. She had tasted the apple and her heart pounded now with a new fear, of discovery.

"Abigail smiled and patted Martha's shoulder. "My father lived to see the first one burn. He didn't hold with witches. He said that, by their judgments, he'd be a witch himself."

Abigail laughed softly, the sweet sound close to Martha's ear. Then they heard horsehoofs approaching on the road below, and they held each other tightly.

A dozen riders, crowding one another on the small road, kicked clouds of dirt around the blazing torches in their hands. There was a boistrous sound to them, rowdy and excited. Martha could hear the low rumble of their laughter.

"Farm hands," Abigail whispered, "they're a rough gang; I'm afraid when I hear them pass on Saturdays. They carry flasks of elderberry, and a peddler told me that they rode onto Captain Brown's land and took his youngest daughter off. Nobody's seen her since . . . When my father was alive, he sat vigil at our door, holding his ax for protection, when they passed. I always hide now when I hear them coming. Sometimes they call out to me as they go by. They know a girl's alone there now; the peddlers tell everything."

"I should think the Elders would burn them. They look like a dozen devils on the loose."

"They're men. Their souls are sacred." Abigail said softly, and pressed her face against Martha's warm neck. Martha shuddered, feeling the girl's hot breath against her flesh, and yet she couldn't move away.

"We'll live high on the hill, well hidden, Martha. We have nothing to fear from them. We're not witches."

"I was born a bastard."

"You have two eyes and no tail that I've seen." Abigail rubbed Martha's arms, warming them.

78

"*I gave birth to a bastard, too.*"

"*And he's no devil.*"

They sat closely, holding each other, cheeks, breasts and thighs pressed as though their joining would protect them from all harm . . .

They saw the funnel of black smoke first, then the flames,—searing the starlit summer sky above the village. Holding tighter, pressed bosom trembling bosom, they wept as the witches burned, each silently imagining the hideous pain of blistering flesh, roasting on human bone.

Drifting later in a nightmare half-sleep, they were silent until they heard the shouts below them on the road. Sitting up, their arms still around each other, they saw the ruffians dismount from their horses and swarm onto the wooden porch of the Richmond tenant farm house.

"*They're looking for you.*" Martha whispered in Abigail's ear, feeling the dark girl's shoulders tremble. Martha pulled her close as though she were protecting her from the assault below.

Three figures charged the plank door and it flew open. Through the uncurtained windows, the women saw the men run through the five rooms, shouting, laughing, growling with disappointment when at last they came out on the porch again, empty-handed. They mounted noisily and galloped off, the last rider hurling an angry torch onto the wooden porch.

By daybreak, the house was burned to the ground, embers pulsing red against the breaking of the grey dawn.

They slept then, the two women wrapped in one another, until the first warmth of the sun broke through the dawn to penetrate their bodies.

Cynthia, half-dreaming that Dave's arms were holding her, and, as they sometimes did in sleep, nearly suffocating her, pulled away and sat upright. "It's hot."

She felt the bed of pine needles under her before she opened her eyes. Looking at Angela, squirming to wakefulness as though the wiggling of her body would shed the skin of sleep, Cynthia remembered. The memory flooded her; her skin chilled and tightened in defense against the horror.

"Oh, my God." Angela said softly, sitting up. She ran her fingers slowly through her long, dark hair, scattering pine needles across her shoulders and her legs. "Oh, my God."

They looked at each other then, knowing where they'd been together, sensing the path that lay ahead of them and that it was too late now to turn back.

Below them at the foot of the hill, beyond the main road, brambles and berry vines tangled thick across the buried foundation of the cremated tenant farm house. Only the broken remains of a brick chimney broke above the burial ground, a monument to the night of terror they had relived.

Apart from each other, isolated by their thoughts, they walked uphill and crawled into their own separate beds an hour before the children woke.

Red Richmond, an early riser, saw the women from his bedroom window as they walked up the hill, rumpled, slump-shouldered with too little sleep. He scratched his chin through the tight tangle of his beard and wondered where they'd been so early in the morning. Even disheveled, Angela was beautiful, and Red vowed he'd make another visit to the hill at the children's naptime.

As Angela prepared breakfast, Cynthia showered, letting the warm water flood her body, hoping to take the chill of the past night away. But the cold nightmare terror went deeper than her flesh, and it was with her as she dressed and hurried down the staircase to the kitchen.

She went straight to the canvasboard, propped carefully against the headboard in the old room. In her mind she could see clearly what she'd planned to paint, the old room as it was now, lifeless and abandoned. But before she focused on the charcoal sketch, she knew what she would find—the old room young and filled with life, the pallet on the floor, the sampler on the wall, the stew pot simmering above the fire.

Pete tottered into the room and stood beside her, his arms clasped tight around her thigh. He smiled.

"That's my bed," he said primly, and pointed to the

80

sketched outline of the pallet, *"but where's my friend, my yellow dog?"*

When Cynthia didn't answer right away, Pete turned and darted from the room, through the kitchen, out the screen door, calling *"Yellow! Yellow!"*

Angela stood in the doorway, staring past Cynthia's shoulder at the charcoal sketch. She also smiled. *"Even with one plate, we've still made a home."*

Janet got up from the kitchen table, her coloring book under her arm, and approached Angela.

"We have lots of plates, Angela, in the cupbaord."

But Angela didn't answer. She drifted further into the old room, her glance locked with Cynthia's.

"Mommy?"

Janet stood on one foot, then the other, frightened, frustrated.

"Mommy, I'm going swimming by myself."

She waited; still no answer. Angela moved closer to her mother, and took Cynthia's hand.

"You don't care if I drown!" Janet ran from the kitchen, crying, flinging her cotton haltar to the grass, kicking off her shorts, and heading naked for the pond.

The women sat together on the window sill, Cynthia stroking Angela's dark hair with gentle motions, both content in the sun.

"I was remembering how you wept when you broke our other plate."

Abigail smiled shyly and looked down toward the floor.

Martha cupped her chin and made her look up again. *"It was no tragedy, my love. We're even closer, sharing one plate now."*

"I've erred twice," Abigail said softly, examining Martha's hand with her fingers, exploring the crevices, the lines and calluses in the palm, *"I've broken your plate and nearly drowned your son. You have much patience to let me stay."*

Martha pressed her lips against the firmness of Abigail's young cheek. *"I haven't much patience, but I have much love."*

This was not, Martha knew, the same feeling that she

81

shared with the peddler who fathered Jeremiah. It was a different feeling, bubbling unheralded from a deeper spring, but it called up in her the same need for warmth and nearness. Hugging Abigail's lithe body to her full breasts, Martha fancied somehow that they could blend and merge into one richer, fuller being. As the two rough-hewn planks hard-nailed together in the center of the cabin formed a stronger ridgepole, so she and Abigail, their arms entwined, their bodies pressed thigh to thigh, formed a woman strong enough to fend off any danger.

The boy frolicked with the yellow dog under the stand of pines, and the women sternly warned him to play close to the cabin before they walked downhill, their hands clasped loosely, toward the bank of golden wildflowers along the creekbed.

"*My mother said no proper lady would remove all her clothing and bathe naked. One should wash underneath the garment, she said.*" Abigail was stripping off her skirt and apron, unbuttoning her blouse, as she babbled gaily, so full of words and new excitement that her talking wouldn't stop. "*It was an argument between them, my mother and my father. My father,*" Abigail snickered as she dropped her blouse and let her young breasts burst free into the sunlight, "*would remove his clothing, every stitch, on summer afternoons, and leap into this cold creek like a frog. Mother was scandalized.*"

"*I often bathe here naked,*" Martha said, trying to match Abigail's easy, conversational tone of voice, but feeling shy, uncomfortable, about removing her long skirt and long-sleeved blouse, although the clothing held the summer heat against her body and caused an itch that covered her all over. She'd seen her body in the dark reflecting waters of the creek throughout the years, and knew it no longer had the firmness of Abigail's body. Martha's breasts were full and hung now from motherhood, her belly was no longer flat against her hip's, having given birth to a child.

"*Come in, it's wonderful!*"

Abigail's white nakedness disappeared under the water and she smiled, only her shoulders and head showing, at Martha on the shore.

"*You mustn't look.*" Martha turned her back to Abigail's

young laughing face, and timidly unhooked the waistband of her heavy skirt.

"*I'm not a witch,*" Abigail called, her voice smiling, "*I won't take your soul!*"

But when Martha dropped her clothing and turned toward the creek, she felt Abigail's look move over her, the need and warmth growing hot and hard inside her, and she thought her soul was lost.

"*I love you,*" Abigail repeated, her face burrowed in the warmth between Martha's naked breasts, "*I love you.*"

They lay together on the creekbank, their legs intertwined, the openness of Martha's womanhood pressed hot and warm against Alibgail's invading thigh. They had no words for what they'd done together, suckling each other's breasts, fondling one another with fingers and exploring lips. They had followed all their needs and feelings, and they had led each other to completeness.

"*I love you, Martha.*"

Martha pressed her lips full on the girl's and found a pathway for her tongue between her teeth.

"*I love you, Abigail,*" she said, when their lips parted, "*I've loved no one as I love you.*"

"*Don't tremble, Martha. God is love and God is good, so love is good.*"

Martha nodded soberly. "*It would seem to follow.*"

"*Our Lord Jesus was himself falsely persecuted. And he was good.*"

"*He was.*"

"*So what do we have to fear?*"

Martha smiled and moved on top of her lover, covering the dark girl's face with soft kisses, tracing the outline of her neck and shoulders with her tongue. But as she heard the girl's pleasured sigh reverberate against her face, she trembled. A picture of the screaming women, branded as witches, floated through her mind. She thought of the old Granny applying leeches to a dying boy. Perhaps the Granny was no witch, perhaps the leeches came too late, perhaps the Granny didn't disappear, but drowned in the deep riptides of the bay.

"*Oh, yes, my love.*" Abigail's fingers pressed against

Martha's scalp and urged her on. Martha's love was too great, her need too rampant and unleashed, to stop the journey of her lips across her lover's naked body.

Afterward, Abigail lay on her back, the noon sun darting through the leaves and splotching her naked body with gold. She closed her eyes against the light; she was content for the first time in her life. She'd wondered what it was to love another person, she'd played in fantasy with loving young Squire Richmond. He had an eye for her, she knew that, she saw the glint, the wiggle of his red mustache when he rode with his father to the farm to load produce for marketing. He was in a class beyond her, of wealth and breeding, and much too proper to break easily through social barriers. His intentions toward her couldn't be honorable; she felt sure of that, and she had no more than a casual interest in him. He'd served as fantasy on lonely afternoons.

There would be no more lonely afternoons for Abigail; she stroked Martha's hair, Martha's head resting against her shoulder. Abigail needed no young man now, no honorable intentions, she'd found love and happiness beyond her expectations. She'd never heard of such a love before, but it was right and fine. She cherished it and thanked God silently.

It was Martha who, as she drifted off to warm sleep on Abigail's soft shoulder, felt a tremor in the recess of her belly, an intangible precognition of what lay beyond their love.

Angela woke first, realizing her nakedness, feeling the weight of Cynthia's head against her shoulder. She lay quite still, a prisoner behind the bars of sunlight, remembering what had gone before.

A perfect pairing, she thought, Abigail and me. She wants what I want. And Angela, who'd dreamed of lying in a woman's arms all of her life, caressed Cynthia's cheek and shoulder, kissed her hair and dreaded the moment when Cynthia would wake.

Cynthia's eyes were open when Angela's lips pressed against her scalp. Alert and tense, as though she'd been awakened by a sense of imminent danger, her mind replayed Martha and Abigail, their tryst. For the first time since she'd welcomed this strange possession, Cynthia was frightened for herself.

She twisted away roughly and sat, her back to Angela. She was mortified with the memory of what had happened.

When Angela summoned the courage to speak, she whispered, trying not to break the spell of closeness that surrounded them.

"It wasn't us," she said, "it was them. Please don't be frightened."

She wanted to reach out and stroke the bare back, touch the soft shoulders, kiss the tense neck, until Cynthia turned and merged against her. She was frightened of rejection and did nothing. She could hear her own sharp, nervous breathing above the rustling of the leaves.

"I'm not frightened," Cynthia answered finally, but her back stiffened further and she leaned forward, creating greater space between her naked body and Angela's. "It won't happen again."

Angela's mind tumbled with terrifying thoughts. Suppose she wants to leave here now, go back to the city, run from the old room, abandon Abigail and Martha?

"They need us." Her voice was a plea, not for two dead women but for herself.

She saw Cynthia sigh, her back heaving as she placed her forehead in her hands. "I know," Cynthia said slowly. "They don't want to let us go."

A smile began somewhere in the core of Angela and spread across her body, tingling her limbs and scalp and cheeks. She would fight for their existence, Martha and Abigail's. As long as they were in control, she and Cynthia loved.

Cynthia dressed quickly, wordlessly, and walked ahead of Angela, stalking angrily up the narrow roadway. She single-mindedly thought of Dave, as she pushed with long strides up the hill; his mouth on hers, his penis filling her.

"Mommy!" Pete, tagged by the yellow dog, tumbled toward her down the roadway.

"Mommy, Janet went swimming at the pond all by herself!" He stuck his lower lip out and put both hands on his hips, indignant.

Cynthia turned, a flash of fear across her face. "Angela!"

Angela broke into a run, passing Cynthia and Pete, racing beyond the roadway, through the thicket, toward the pond.

Chapter Seven

Janet had every intention of drowning, but her swimming lessons at the Y served her too well. Punishing her mother was not strong enough motivation to keep her legs from treading water when she began to sink. Her will to live outweighed self-pity; she sat on the grassy bank and pouted, until she felt the noon sun high above her head.

If she couldn't drown, surely she could get lost, and hordes of men with flashlights and helicopters would spend days above the hillside, looking for her. Her mother would clutch her stomach, squeeze tears out of her eyes, go sleepless for nights, and beg a television reporter to offer a reward for Janet's safe return.

She walked into the shadows of the pines and tried to disappear, but every time she thought, delightedly, that she'd succeeded in getting lost, she caught a glimpse of the brick chimney beside the house, or of Red's cabin nestled in the woods. Finally she found a place from which she could see nothing familiar. She made a cushion of pine needles in the shade and sat down. Although she knew she couldn't be far from home, she vowed now that she wouldn't move until her mother found her.

Cynthia ran wild along the creekbed calling, "Janet! Janet!" Janet snickered in her fist, and nestled closer to the tree. She saw a flash of bare legs, Angela's; Janet curled into an embryo and didn't breathe until she'd passed.

Cynthia finally sat, worn and breathing hard, on the front porch, her arms protectively around her son. Pete's chubby fingers were entwined in the matted ruff of Yellow Dog, assuring himself that the mongrel wouldn't run away.

"Angela!"

Angela was loping, weary from hard running, up the roadway toward the house.

"Red Richmond knows these woods," Cynthia yelled, "Get him. Maybe he can find her."

Angela sighed and nodded. She turned and walked, as quickly as her aching legs would carry her, down the roadway toward the cabin at its foot.

But when she saw him, in jeans and a t-shirt, red beard glinting in the sunlight outside his cabin, he wasn't Red at all.

"I thought I heard a voice on the hill. I prayed that it was you; I prayed God kept you safe."

It wasn't concern about his father's property that had led Squire Richmond to ride to the tenant farm and look into the damage from the fire. He'd searched the rubble thoroughly, kicking blackened windowframes and doors aside, hefting scarred beams still warm from flame. He'd seen no sign of human remains and he'd set out to search the woods. His heart was high at the sight of the girl, unharmed.

"The burnings bring out the worst in people. The farmhouse is in ashes, a great loss to my father. He'll have to build again before he'll find a tenant for the farm."

Abigail nodded, averting her eyes. She hadn't meant to encounter Squire Richmond. Filled with love, bubbling with new excitement, she'd merely meant to walk the woods alone while Martha fed the boy, to pick a nosegay, perhaps, for Martha's hand.

"Still in all, it isn't such a tragedy. You escaped the fire."

Squire Richmond smiled shyly. Unlike his older brothers, he was not equipped to pay court coldly to a proper lady, and marry merely to enhance the family standing, or fortune. A romantic, Squire wrote poetry while his brothers hunted squirrels, sang soft ballads while his father tended the property and governed the pious village. Squire gave his father reason for concern.

"He'll be a preacher. That's all he's fit for." His father had said publicly, thanking God for the bounty of his other four, fit sons. When he'd seen his youngest son go moonstruck at the sight of the darkhaired tenant farmer's daughter, the Elder Richmond had forbad Squire to pay her court. The father knew, when Squire had begged to evaluate the damage at the tenant farm this morning, that the boy was more concerned with the girl's fate than with the depreciation of the property. The other boys were needed at their daily tasks and the Elder Richmond had his hands full in the village, so he had let Squire go.

The ridding of a few witches had billowed, beyond control, into a scourge. The village, like a pack of wild dogs with the scent of blood, cried for the smell of burning flesh. The Elder Richmond, not as God-fearing as he showed himself to be, knew the current burnings were more vendetta than witch-hunt, but he knew, too, that he must please the villagers, who gave him power and on whose labor he accumulated profit. More politic than pious, the Elder Richmond held daily public councils and kept his decisions in rhythm with the excited pounding of the village pulse. They wanted witches, he would give them witches and kneel beside them as the flesh burned, thankful for deliverance.

The Elder Richmond owned the land beyond the village on the West and South sides. He owned the narrow shops in the village square where blacksmiths and bakers plied their trades and paid their leases to him. He owned three of the four piers in the harbor, and collected cargo fees from docking ships. In effect, he owned the village, and he felt it his responsibility to manage it, to keep its people satisfied. The Elder Richmond never shied from duty and he knew that religious fervor served as a placebo for the harsh, hard reality of building a new world.

Burnings could do no harm, he reasoned. Only women suffered, and their pain could be no greater than the pain of birth, God's own judgment against their sex. There was some question, as he knew from the papers that arrived aboard ship from England, that the female of the species possessed a soul greater than a cow's or hen's. It was the Elder Richmond's theory that, should witches exist (and he was not at all clear on this point), they must be female, their souls such small and weak prey for the devil. He knew that in England, women burned and hung for witchcraft, but he'd heard a peddler's story that in Salem, only half a year ago, a man had been pressed to death between two planks for witchery. Richmond hoped the villagers had not heard the loose-mouthed peddler's fancy. He didn't want to suffer the binding of his conscience should he have to lash a man to the charred stake in the square.

The sensitive young Squire Richmond listened to his father when he sat at public council. He found much meaning between his father's words. Consequently, Squire, a poet and balladeer, didn't believe in witches, or, for that matter, in the sanctity of Jesus Christ.

"Black as nesting ravens, the covy of her curls, and, quick as flight, her love escapes my gaze." Abigail looked up at Squire; his eyes were as bold a blue as the sky.

"A poem I wrote," he smiled nervously, *"for you."*

She shrugged, half-smiled, *"Thank you."*

"Where will you go now? This is no time for a young woman to be travelling the roads."

"My father taught me many things, and I'll manage."

Squire Richmond smiled broadly, and glanced up at the crest of the pine studded hill. *"You've found the bastard's cabin. It must be in poor repair."*

"I can make it do."

"Did you find their remains, the old woman and her daughter? My brothers longed to climb up to the cabin and set it off, for sport, but my mother is so firmly convinced it's damned by God, I believe she's even frightened my father."

Squire laughed. Abigail smiled but didn't answer.

"You'll be alone there. You may starve in the winter, or freeze without sufficient firewood. Have you got an ax, at least?"

She nodded.

"You're brave as well as beautiful."

She blushed and turned away from him. He caught her chin in his fingers and studied her flushing face.

"I'm not a ruffian, you know. I've no talent for accumulating riches. I'm not religious, either."

"I have a feeling you're a good man and you'll do well by life," she said politely, wishing he'd release her chin.

"I need such faith," he answered softly, and leaned his face towards hers.

She pulled away and walked a few feet from him.

"I don't wish to frighten you," he said reverently and with respect. *"I see that you're a proper girl."*

She nodded, staring at the ground, hoping that he'd leave. She heard the warm, low rumble of his laugh.

"Then I expect I'll have to act in proper manner, too, won't I?"

She nodded again and stiffened as she heard him walking toward her, pine needles snapping underneath his boots.

"I'm Squire Richmond."

"I know that."

"I know you know; I'm hoping to do things properly between us. May I know your name?"

"Abigail," she whispered, afraid not to answer him, *"Abigail Landry."*

He touched her shoulder lightly, briefly. She could hear a smile of happiness when he spoke. *"I'll be proper, Abigail, I grant you that."*

She didn't look again until his steps were far off and she could only see branches tremble above him as he pushed a path downhill. He whistled, more sharply and musically than any bird, a song of joy; it replayed itself until she found she was humming the same notes, walking home.

"Angela!"

She heard Red's voice and turned to watch him chase after her up the hill.

He planted himself, hulking and out of breath, in front of her. "What happened to us?"

Angela smiled. "Nothing. I came to ask if you'd help us find Janet."

"Janet?"

Red's mind was spinning with weird images, with words he thought he'd said to a strange old-fashioned girl he'd never met.

"She's wandered off, Red, we're afraid she's lost."

Red shook his head and ran his fingers through his hair, as though he could comb out the remnants of his waking dream, unsnarl the puzzling tangles.

"Nothing happened between us?"

"When?"

91

"Just now, down by the cabin."

Angela took his arm and led him up the hill. She didn't know how to explain it, and she wasn't sure that he could understand.

"No, nothing happened. Come on, Cynthia's worried."

As he searched for the overgrown footpaths of his boyhood explorations, he tried to reconstruct the conversation in his mind. It made no sense. But, moving quietly in the brush, pine cones crushing under his work boots, he had the feeling that he'd searched these woods before, looking for a girl.

"Janet!"

He called the name loudly, hoping the noise would shoo away the lingering feeling that something had invaded him, was fighting him for self-control.

"Janet! Dammit, you can't be lost up here. Every path leads back to the house. Stop playing games, kid, you're scaring your mother!"

His voice wound around the tree trunks and Janet grinned, pressed hard against the bark and out of sight. She was glad she scared her mother. Scared; that meant her mother cared. For once, she thought in great self-satisfaction, Pete wasn't the center of attention. She scarcely breathed for fear she would be found.

Chapter Eight

Cynthia avoided the old room, sending Pete to the kitchen to make his own lunch. It was a kamikaze tactic, but she chose to chance a mess of bread crumbs, smears of peanut butter, and spilt milk, in preference to possession by the old room.

Pete had mixed feelings about the assignment. Was he being charged with responsibility, or was he being shunted, his pivotal position in the household sabotaged by his lost sister? Confused, he didn't spill a drop of milk, but he wiped peanut butter off his hands across the kitchen table. That took care of both contingencies.

He liked the game that they were playing, all of them but Janet. It was no different than playing astronaut, recreating space movies that he'd seen on TV. He knew Janet was furious because she wasn't in the game. He couldn't help it if she didn't know how to play.

He liked the yellow dog far better, anyhow; it didn't boss him all the time. He chewed a gooey hunk of peanut butter sandwich and soaked it in milk inside his mouth until it decomposed and slid slimey down his throat.

On the front porch, Cynthia sat and stared downhill, half focusing on Red's voice calling Janet, until the name, constantly repeated, sounded unreal. Cynthia was only vaguely worried about the girl. She trusted Janet's intelligence and resourcefulness. The hill was not so large as to be dangerous, no bears ran wild, and nightfall was still half an afternoon away.

Years ago she'd read a number of books about homosexuality, in her effort to become a sophisticated New Yorker. She gave to GAA and once wrote a letter to Bella supporting Gay Rights legislation. In the agency Dave had worked for before, two of his coworkers had been homosexuals; a third was a lesbian. Cynthia'd had them over for cocktails at Christmas. She'd felt delight and pride then in her liberalism, just as she'd been thrilled in college to take a black student home for Easter to her all white home town in Montana.

Never before had she considered what homosexuals did, or why. If she'd been pressed to elaborate on her academic knowledge of homosexuality, she would surely have stated, "it's the same as being straight, only your choice of mate is different." How educated, experienced, that sounded; but now she knew it couldn't be dismissed so glibly.

Cynthia certainly understood closeness between women. She'd bonded with her mother, to survive; she'd bonded with her college girlfriends, to sustain the onslaughts of aggressive young men. She'd learned to tease and toy, to control and manipulate, the protective devices that were mainstays of her midwestern upbringing, meant to protect virginity until the proper man was found, or until curiosity became too overbearing to resist. Maintaining control over sexual byplay was the base of a woman's power, Cynthia was taught, and friendship with girlfriends became home base; the only time a girl could relax and be herself. While some girls viewed their friends as competition in the mighty battle for a man, Cynthia and her crowd had clung together for mutual support in the face of the fray. She liked women, always had. Her fondest memories of schooldays hung on girlish secrets, giggling spend-the-nights, sharing dreams and insecurities. She'd played touch football, girls against the boys, and revelled when the Girl's Art Club received more scholarships than the boy's group did. She'd held girlfriends to comfort them, and hugged fondly at pajama parties, but never had the thought of sexual fulfillment with a woman crossed her mind.

She couldn't make sense of her own ambivalence. For Martha and for Abigail, the lesbian relationship was right, was necessary—the sense of wholeness as they meshed one in the other—but to use her, Cynthia, to resurrect it, to trap two living women in the tight web of the dead ones' needs, was immoral, despicable, frightening. Cynthia, still on the porch steps and staring downhill, raged at Martha, locked now inside of her. But Martha sat tight, stoic, smiling, waiting; Cynthia placed her forehead in her hands and tried to push back her panic so she could understand.

Woman-woman was not the same as woman-man. There were no devices, no tactics, no ammunition that the other didn't have as well. No excuses served as camouflage; the battle for each other was fought unarmed, head-on. She expected more from a woman than from a man and, recognizing this, Cynthia was stunned.

Dave was tired, but Angela was lazy. Dave, clumsy; Angela, careless. Dave had his mind on important matters, but Angela was simply inattentive. Cynthia demanded no less of Angela than she demanded of herself.

And in the act of love, she and Dave came close together, parted and returned and parted, two hands applauding. Martha and Abigail (*she and Angela;* Cynthia winced, embarrassed, remembering), were two hands clasped.

Angela did not look into Cynthia's eyes romantically, as Dave did. She looked through them, past them, into the dark and vulnerable place beyond. There was no hiding from a woman, and Cynthia trembled, afraid of that dark and previously inviolate place which Angela had invaded; Cynthia was unable to remember what she'd hidden there.

Angela sat on the back steps, watching Red's shadowed profile moving in the brush . . . . She had carefully avoided all literature on homosexuality, and had walked the long way around to her classes when gay picket lines appeared on campus. She knew too well the feelings in her, and had postponed the inevitable confrontation with the reality of her needs. She was grateful to Abigail, locked now inside of her, for having the courage to live out her fantasies.

She liked Red better than most men, but then she'd never been in close proximity to any man except her father. The adolescents who'd tried to fondle her on her few dates were something less than human in her mind.

Her father's method of survival, in a noisy, hostile world,

was to yell the loudest—"I'll kill the bastard if he fucks around with me!" "I'll kill the sonofabitch who touches you!"—when, in fact (and Angela had seen this very early), everyone pushed him around, and yelling was his only form of protest.

He'd had great half circles of sweat beneath his arms when he'd gotten off from work, and he'd lift his small daughter, in the rancid air surrounding him, to rub her tender cheek against the black, stubble of his beard. In those growing up years, though she knew he tried to love her and to support her as best he could, she felt she was a favored prisoner in a concentration camp, the smell of sweat, the constant references to "Kill!" making her daily more dubious about her future.

In school, Angela had seen males as pushers. One pushed, another pushed back, a third would push them both, roughhousing in the hallways. Although some girls squealed and cheered in admiration, Angela felt safer when she neared an exit. Boys weren't the same as she, with sweat triangles on their backs, and long fuzz that appeared sporadically among their pimples. They seemed to know the answers to all the vast and puzzling questions (like who they were, why they were here, and where they might be going), and it wasn't until her first year at college that Angela discovered this male knowledge to be a clever sham.

She loved her father in some faraway, forbidden way. He could have left her, a small girl, to her own devices, dependent on bureaucracy for her survival. Instead, he chose to dedicate his life to working at a job he loathed and brought his meager earnings home every Saturday to pay for their food and rent. He would have killed for her, perhaps, because she was his property, his responsibility, and he was a man of pride.

She could hardly wait to graduate, to come of age, so she could find a place that was her own, devoid of that male smell, the bathroom free of sweat socks in the hamper and the strong thick musk of male urine that seemed to hover possessively in every corner. Her father had protested perfunctorarily—"I'll kill your landlord if he bothers you!"—but the fact was, Angela knew, that her father was relieved,

96

bone-weary, from displaying strength for her—"One of those egghead professors lays a hand on you, I'll murder the bum!"—and he relished the freedom, alone in his small apartment, to drink beyond capacity and pass out on the sofa, his only escape from a threatening world.

They both were prisoners of their genders, he trapped by maleness, she by femaleness. In a dogpack, Angela once read, weak males must be followers or they are disemboweled by the others. The females have a choice; to follow the male leader for protection, or to stop running and bond together, establishing a territory in which to live and rear their pups without the migrating chaos, but where they will, eventually, fall prey to other packs of marauding males. There is no guarantee of safety, in any case, except for the male leader of the pack. And even he is fated, finally, to fall at the jaws of a younger, stronger male.

At this moment, unknown to Angela, her father lay, drunk, in the Bronx, a pool of vomit drying at his side; he'd been held up by a mugger and told by his boss, sneeringly, that the lost receipts would be deducted from his paycheck. "A man has to be tough to drive a hack, Lucenti. You got to know how to take care of yourself." The mugger'd had a gun, for crissakes, the mugger'd had a gun!

Had Angela known of this, it would have underscored her gut reaction to the world. She didn't want to run in the protective cluster of a pack. Its violence and rules were beyond her understanding. She'd rather take her chances hidden in the woods, bonded with her own sex for survival. That, at least, she thought she understood.

She listened to Red calling Janet, a protective male herding the progeny into the pack. She was angry at herself for asking Red to help. She'd brought a man into their woman-thing and he'd assert himself now; it was his nature.

Sitting on the back porch steps, Angela remembered each moment of the creekbank encounter, savoring it step by step. She'd dreamed of how it would be, woman and woman, but no dream held the magnificence of that reality. Her imagination had been too limited. To merge, to find one's self and double it, twice gentle, twice needing, twice whole. To watch your shadow, long in the morning, shorten and slip into yourself at midday. . . .

Even then, in mid-afternoon, Angela cast no shadow. She was in love.

Red felt a stirring, too, as he stood in the coolness of the pines, casting futile searching glances for the girl. He'd had a number of girls in his young life, from the thrill seekers at his private school in Boston, who only wanted to see a real-life erection and, their curiosity satiated, sent him home with aching gonads, to his college steady, who doled out sex in trade for movie tickets and dinners at off-campus restaurants. In the Vermont commune where he'd lived half a year, the sexual operative was indiscrimination, what turned you on and where and when; no residual responsibility. It didn't work for Red. If he enjoyed a liason, he wanted to romance the girl, to carry wood for her, to bring her flowers, to protect her from the advances of other men. Possession was against the commune rules and no man there could cope with it for long. The commune was always transient except for the two women who owned the farmland, seemingly as permanently entrenched as the posts which served as strong foundations for the building. Those women, too, took men from time to time, and had, between them, seven children whose fathers names they'd probably forgotten. In Europe, Red had biked from France to Italy and had a flash affair with a student artist from the States. When she thought that she was pregnant by him, she hurried home to Palo Alto, California, where she had a fiancé, she said, waiting and ready for the ceremony. Red fantasized that the fiancé was dark, just like the girl, and reveled in the hope that she'd brought forth a fair-skinned, red-headed baby, to her unsuspecting husband's dismay.

Since Europe, Red hadn't met a girl who'd brought forth his protective feelings, who'd given rise in him the sense that, with her at his side, the world was his to conquer—until he saw the darkhaired sleepy Angela, vacationing on the hill above him, shy and slender, unequipped to fight the hostile forces of the world alone. Red needed someone to need him. He thought that perhaps because his belly tightened when he thought of her, because he felt stronger, surer when she walked next to him, because he wanted to delight her with gifts and shield her from hurt, he must be falling in love. His groin tightened and he lost his irritation at the missing child.

"Janet," he called loudly, confidently, in the thick woods, "Janet, honey, don't be frightened, Red will find you!"

He knew that Angela could hear his voice.

By late afternoon Cynthia stood at the wood's edge, shifting her weight nervously, feeling the approach of night. She had a hundred fantasies: her daughter drowned or crushed beneath a fallen branch, her daughter with a broken leg or arm, having tumbled from a tree, her daughter the victim of a red fox or mountain rattler, her daughter kidnapped, gagged and raped.

She knew from the hard lessons of her childhood that a woman must give a man a chance to do the saving, the protecting, and that if he fails, she must stand ready to do the job herself. She moved into the woods; Cynthia didn't notice Angela watching from the back porch, then following a discreet distance from her.

"Janet, baby."

Janet, nestled nearby beneath her tree, smiled and held her breath. It was worth it, every minute of hiding, even the red earthworm that had crawled across her bare rump, it was worth it to hear her mother call her "baby."

"Honey, if you can hear me, answer. Mommy's worried about you."

Not yet. Janet pressed her cheeks between her knees. Not yet. Perhaps she'd stay out here all night; then they'd all look for her and leave Pete in the house alone, frightened of the dark. Maybe he'd fall out of bed and hurt himself, maybe he'd run away to get even and they'd never find him. Maybe the yellow dog would grow hungry and eat him, or a snake would choke him like in the Tarzan movies. Maybe Mommy would call Daddy and he'd leave his work and come to Massachusetts early, crying out Janet's name and walking with his flashlight through the woods, although he hated woods and was openly afraid of snakes.

"Janet!"

"Janet!"

Red's voice from one side, Mommy's from the other. Janet was surrounded by people wanting her. She smiled with closed lips, happy, and fell asleep against the rough bark of the tree, to the musical litany of her own name.

Chapter Nine

They were not deep in the woods; snatches of white clapboard, the siding of the house, could still be glimpsed through overhanging branches. Angela followed quietly, their footsteps barely audible on the pine-crushed earth. When Cynthia stood still and leaned against the rough bark of a cedar, waiting, Angela's pace slowed, and she took careful steps, feeling alone and frightened, approaching Cynthia's back as though it were a wall between them. They were less than twenty feet from where Janet lay sleeping underneath a tree, but neither woman thought of Janet then; she wasn't part of Abigail's and Martha's world.

"Don't turn away from me. I've done nothing that should hurt you, Martha."

"A rich young man is courting you. You're a mortal woman, and not stupid."

"I never said that he was courting! I only mentioned meeting him. It was a chance encounter."

"You'll meet him again. You're no fool!"

"I love you."

"Then you are a fool. I've nothing here to give you; no land, no babies I can offer."

Abigail reached out and placed her hands quite softly on Martha's shoulders. She saw the tremble that her touch sent through Martha's body; then Martha's spine stiffened, her shoulders seemed to shrug Abigail off.

"I regret the day I asked you in." The words were bitter, loud enough to dam the threatening tears. *"I trusted you, and now you'll deceive me."*

Abigail did not remove her hands, although she felt the muscles of Martha's shoulders tightening, rejecting comfort. *"I told him nothing about you or the boy. Like the villagers, he believes you're dead."*

"He'll come here for you, and he'll see the boy."

Abigail laughed gently and pressed her cheek against Martha's hard, stiff shoulder. *"Why should he come for me? I'm a tenant farmer's daughter. I have no dowry. His father wouldn't stand for it."*

"You see? You hope he does!"

Abigail shook Martha gently, feeling the flare of jealousy, as though she'd stepped too close to a flame. Martha's skin was hot and dry; she held her body rigid to prevent the trembling.

Abigail stroked the nape of Martha's neck. It was damp beneath the tangled fall of hair, sticky with the August heat.

"I have no interest in Squire Richmond, I have no interest in Squire Richmond, I have no interest . . . ."

"He'll be back. He's seen your beauty."

"I have no interest in Squire Richmond, I have no interest in . . . ."

"You'll go with him. You'll do what women do. I know you will. I did it with the peddler myself."

Jealousy sparked and flushed through Abigail. Martha had intended it. *"And you found joy in it, didn't you?"*

Martha smiled slightly, defiant.

"Didn't you?" Abigail's voice trembled; her mind filled with fantasies of a peddler's calloused fingers moving on Martha's naked flesh. *"Did you love him?"*

Martha could not maintain the pretense, though the reaction that it brought in Abigail gave her some small, ugly satisfaction. *"I didn't love him, Abigail, not as I love you."*

They turned into each other and held close, lovers pressing breasts and bellies, hips and thighs so tightly that the world could not squeeze in between them.

"If he should come, I'll send him scatting." Abigail's tears warmed Martha's neck and spread into the fabric of her dress.

"When I was small," Martha said softly, her lips brushing Abigail's ear with each word, *"I dreamed I'd leave this hilltop. My mother told me about the village, drew pictures of the houses and the shops, in ash across the hearth, so I*

could see. I dreamed a young man in fine breeches and a leather hat would climb this hill, adventuring, and find me. He'd be proper and landed, of course, a gentleman and servant of the Lord, and, in a speech so glorious that night-birds would sing in the afternoon, he'd declare his honorable intentions. I'd live inside the village then, in a fine house with tight walls that kept out the winter wind. I'd have a feather bed and sculptured chairs, and pots and kettles, and children, everything in plenty. The ladies of the church would come to visit, just as my mother said they did in the fine house where she was bonded, and at Sunday meeting I'd sit in the first pew of women, my children proper all around me, and God would love me then." Martha laughed, but there was little joy in it.

Abigail squeezed tighter, Martha in the circle of her arms, as though the pressure of her embrace could drive away the years of pain.

"That was a pretty dream," Abigail said softly, her face cradled in the curve of Martha's neck.

"It could come true for you, my Abby. Squire Richmond might be such a man." Martha sighed and pressed her lips in Abigail's thick, dark hair.

"I love you."

"I'm a woman. I can work and give birth and rear, but men are the keepers of dreams."

"Of that dream. It's a pretty dream, I grant you, but there are others."

They held close for a moment before Martha sighed and broke the embrace.

"We'll live hard here, you and me."

"The boy will grow and help."

Abigail reached for Martha's hand, and they walked slowly, softly, shoulders touching, as they ducked the overhanging branches that led deeper into the woods.

"When Jeremiah's big enough," Martha said, her eyes still washed with tears and the world around her blurred, *"we'll build another room for him. I can fell a tree, you know."*

"And so can I," Abigail smiled proudly, *"my father taught me. I can bring it down without a sound and in the proper place, too."*

103

"We'll need a boy's strength for carrying and splitting."

"Jeremiah's growing fast. I believe I've watched him grow an inch this summer. He'll be tall, like you."

"Do you sew, too?"

Abigail nodded. "Passing well."

"The boy needs breeches. He's been in skirts too long. I'm only a fair sewer, too, not having had the cloth to practice on, but I've got four dresses of my mother's, like this one I'm wearing and I imagine we could pull the seams and make the boy a pair of breeches."

"The dress the boy is wearing was yours?"

"My mother made it for me from one of her own, and I wore it till the day she died. I buried her as God made her, and I wore her dress from then on, until it grew so worn and torn it no longer covered me."

Abigail entwined her fingers loosely with Martha's, leading her toward an open patch between two towering oaks.

"You have four other dresses?"

"I'm saving them. I have no way of getting more. I grant the boy's breeches are important, and we'll use a dress for them, but we should sew them big and hem them wide so he can wear them till he's grown."

Abigail sat underneath one of the giant oaks; she pulled Martha beside her. She shifted, adjusting the long folds of her skirt.

"I've got half a mind to cut this dress of mine, and make it into breeches."

"Abigail!"

"I wore them as a girl; my father thought it practical for hunting and for riding."

"A woman dressed in breeches defies God's will." Martha patted Abigail's arm as though they were compatriots in sin.

"It seems as though God failed to do his duty."

"Abby!"

Abigail grinned, and squeezed Martha's fingers. "If you want Jeremiah to wear breeches, you must provide them. God provided neither breeches nor skirts for his children."

Martha pulled her hand away and looked sharply at her friend. "Don't blaspheme. I won't tolerate it."

104

Abigail's grin widened. *"That's the voice you use when you chastise Jeremiah."*

"I was born in sin and so was Jeremiah. Together, you and I have sinned. Already, God isn't pleased with us."

Abigail gestured above their heads to the multicolored cluster of the oak branch, a jagged outline against the grey dusk sky. *"The birds still sing for us, and give us joy. Squirrels come forth so we can catch and eat them. The sun shines yellow in the morning when you kiss my lips, and at night, when we do the thing you think displeases God, the stars are just as silver over us as over the church steeple in the village."*

"My mother had a Bible, and it was those words I learned to read. I know what pleases and displeases God."

"Oh? God has spoken to you, has he, just as he spoke to those pious village elders who set fire to the witches last night?" Abigail was lovingly sarcastic, and unaware that she was dipping lightly into the dark well of terror inside Martha.

Martha shuddered.

"I believe there is a God," Abigail continued conversationally, *"but he hasn't spoken to me, nor has he spoken to the Village Elders."*

"Abigail!" Martha warned. She felt the same sharp chill of fear she'd known in childhood, reading the stern words by firelight, the world outside the cabin black and still.

"My mother hid books in the lining of her trunk when she came to this country. They told about things that no one mentions here. In Italy, the Christians worship Mary, who was unwed when Jesus was conceived."

Martha removed her hand from Abigail's and clasped her fingers tightly around her own knees. *"We don't worship Mary in the true church. My mother taught me that."*

"Jesus forgave a whore."

"Abigail!"

"You know that. You have his words embroidered on your sampler."

"I didn't know their meaning then. My mother chose those words to teach me stitching the same winter that she died."

"God's words may mean one thing or they may mean

another. My father and my mother said that, both of them. It was the one thing they agreed on." Abigail forced a laugh, hoping to break the barrier that was growing between Martha and herself.

"Some things are clear enough," Martha answered, her jaw set forward stubbornly. *"Timothy said: 'Let woman learn in silence with all subjection. She that liveth in pleasure is dead while she liveth'."*

Abigail moved close then and circled Martha's waist with her arms, placing her face in the valley of Martha's breasts, feeling the quickening of Martha's heart against her cheek. It seemed a long time that she stayed there, neither of them moving, neither speaking. At last, Abigail pulled slowly on the ties that closed Martha's bodice, trying to make no sound as she pushed back the damp material and found the flesh beneath it with her lips. Martha softened then, her body curling to take Abigail's weight against it, her fingers tangling in the long, dark hair and holding tight.

"I read the Bible, too, you know." Abigail's words rose softly, almost imperceptible above the rustling leaves. *" 'Intreat me not to leave thee, or to return from following after thee: for whither thou goest, I will go; and where thou lodgest, I will lodge: thy people shall be my people, and thy God my God: Where thou diest, will I die, and there will I be buried: the Lord do so to me, and more also, if ought but death part thee and me.' "*

Martha took Abigail's face in her hands and lifted it to kiss her lips.

"It was a woman who said that," Abigail whispered, her lips still touching Martha's, *"It was Ruth who said that."*

"I know." Their tongues touched, just the tips. *"Ruth said that to Naomi."*

And as Martha felt their bodies merging, becoming one with mounting pleasure, the long, dark nights of her childhood spent in Bible reading took their toll, and she thought she heard the voice of her mother reading on, Naomi's words to Ruth. *"Sit still, my daughter, until thou know how the matter will fall: for the man will not be in rest, until he have finished the thing this day."*

Janet woke slowly, hearing the drift of women's voices as if in a dream. She also heard some slight movement in the brush beyond, but it was growing dark and she couldn't see anyone.

"Mommy!" The game was over now, and she was frightened.

"Mommy!"

She got no answer, although the murmur and rustle in the brush somewhere beyond continued.

Chapter Ten

Red leaned against a tree trunk, his body heavy with fatigue. He heard the girl call once, then twice. He straightened, held his head still, listening for the source.

"Mommy!"

He turned in the direction of the cry and walked quickly, pushing branches from his face, catching his blue jeans on berry brambles. He heard the fabric of his shirt tear, felt the slap and sting of thorns scraping his skin.

It was a thorn that spun him backward in time, the opening of flesh, the warm, slow flow of blood across his shoulder . . . . Squire Richmond reached to touch the wound, distressed that his best shirt had been torn on the brambles. He'd dressed so carefully, in his finest breeches, and his leather boots shined up with beeswax. He'd made his mind up riding home that afternoon, and had not asked but told his father his intentions, an act requiring courage Squire never believed he had. Love, he thought, builds a man and gives him strength. It was his vision of the dark-haired girl that braced his backbone when he spoke and held his father's look.

"I will marry her."

The announcement was distressing to the Elder Richmond and Squire was surprised his father, while he flinched, offered no argument. A wrinkle formed across the Elder Richmond's brow, the same long wrinkle the Squire had seen appear when his father sat at head of village council and, after some deliberation, pronounced a judgment. But no judgment came; Squire dressed himself in his best suit, and rode back to the hill to take his chosen woman's hand. It was a long walk up the hillside; no horse could weave the path. Squire didn't feel the brambles on

108

that walk up; he dismissed the slapping of his neck and cheeks by branches. His heart was joyous and he sang a song composed of one lone word: *Abigail, Abigail, Abigail.* The name changed every time he sang it, its syllables becoming poems, its rhythm a pure melody.

He called it now, and loudly, no longer musical. The cabin appeared empty and though he saw some movement in the dusk beyond the stand of pines, it seemed to come from a wild yellow dog. Peering in the cabin, he saw it was clean and neat; Abigail had clearly meant to make a home there. He called her name a dozen times, to no response; as the hilltop darkened, his heart quickened with the fear that she was lost or hurt in the woods. He'd heard of hungry foxes attacking humans; he'd seen snakes that slithered from the hilltop in dry weather.

In all his life, Squire Richmond had attained no victory. His brothers bullied him, his father found him lacking. He had no head for making money, and neither the back nor the hands for farming. His poems and ballads had been a family secret; such frivolity was considered ungodly by the village. But Abigail had not turned pale when he'd recited his poetry to her; she'd said (the words repeated in his mind with every footfall) *I have a feeling you're a good man and you'll do well by life.*

He could not lose her; he needed her to live. *"Abigail!"*

Should she be hurt, he'd nurse her. Should she be maimed, he'd still marry her and love her through her pain. Should she be lost and frightened, he would find her, hold her, make her one with him. He could not lose her.

"Abigail!"

He had no faith that there was a God, and yet he prayed then as he ran wildly through the brush. He'd be an Elder like his father, he'd be a minister, he'd never sing or write another poem, if only God would keep her safe until he found her.

"Abigail!"

The women heard the cry too late; he was on them.

Martha ran beyond the trees to hide her naked body. Abigail stood, holding her rumpled dress in front of her.

Squire Richmond did not understand what he had seen; he tried to liken it to the time when he'd caught farm girls

109

bathing naked in the bay, although that was against the rules of every village, and, thcy said, displeasing to the sight of God.

"You are no gentleman!" Abigail screamed at him, her voice wild, beyond control. *"You have no right here!"*

"I have a right here," Squire answered, his face flushed with embarrassment, *"this is my father's land."*

Even so, he turned his back to her. He felt as heated as he had on the day he'd run from the village green out to his father's farm, to prove he was as regular a boy as his brothers . . . . As Abigail had leapt up, he'd seen her breasts, her bare legs, the dark triangle that his brothers had drawn in the sand, to illustrate for him the workings of a woman. The sight of Abigail's young naked body gave rise to an aching below his belly like the one he felt before he wrote a poem. His organ stiffened then, as it did now; he had no writing board to press across his lap, to hide his shame. He pressed his hand against his groin, and knew he could not turn around to face the girl.

"I came to court you, Abigail." The words rang around his ears, and he thought that he would faint before she answered.

"I have no interest in your courting, Squire Richmond."

"My intentions are honorable Abigail. I've told my father that I'll marry you."

"I'll never marry you, Squire Richmond."

Her words held the same tone his father's had. *You'll never have the makings of a man, Squire Richmond.* His mother's words, too. *You sit and moon all day, you're not a natural boy, Squire.* And all his brothers. *You'll never be as strong as I; you'll never take a farm, or land, or a woman.* Resentment boiled in his head, heating up his anger.

"You'll marry me or I'll know why!" His voice was strident, a boy's bravado. He forced himself to turn, his fists placed manfully on his hips; he saw that Agibail was dressed and standing, hand in hand, with the other woman. A stranger, tall and long-limbed, her thick hair uncombed and tangled, the woman looked like pictures he'd seen in the church school of the devil's mistress. Squire swallowed hard and spoke again. *"You can't refuse me. The village*

110

Elders will uphold my right to chose a woman who is not spoken for."

"But I am spoken for." Agibail felt Martha stiffen at her side, and she squeezed her fingers tightly.

"Who speaks for you?" He said defensively, as though no one would deign to speak for Abigil, as though he was being charitable in offering himself.

Martha, angered, spoke sharply, quickly, commandeering his glance with hers, and holding the hostile look between them. *"I speak for her."*

Squire Richmond laughed uncomfortably, not understanding. *"Are you her mother?"*

"No."

"Her sister?"

"No."

"Her cousin?"

"No. I am not blood kin."

Martha felt her face flush and she would have looked down, reluctant to continue the unfair fight, but Abigail's fingers squeezed her own again and gave her courage.

"I'm taking her in marriage." Squire Richmond spoke with condescension, as though explaining to a child. The strange woman was not right, he thought; that was clear. It was his duty to protect his bride from her.

"She is already married, sir." There was no subservience in Martha's words. She pulled Abigail closer to her. Their arms touched, seemed to merge.

"Already married?" Squire Richmond could not believe that this was true. He saw the list of marriages brought forth each week before the village council, and Abigail had never been among them.

"She is married, sir, to me."

It made no sense, it made no sense at all; Squire shook his head and looked again at the two women, arm pressed to arm, hand linked in hand. He stared at Abigail, a pleading in his eyes.

"Women cannot marry."

"We have done so." Abigail spoke directly to him, her chin firm and defiant.

"In what church?"

"In this church," Abigail replied, and motioned to the

111

darkening forest that surrounded them, *"in God's church."*

"This is not a church. The church is in the village, and only annointed clergy can perform the marriage ritual."

"I annointed myself," Martha said sternly. *"I am our clergy."*

She put her arm around Abigail's shoulders then, and, taking Abigail's hand in her own, she pressed their clasped hands in the hollow of her breasts, the classic position of marital possession. All the lessons of the church school filled his mind; the very statements that he had believed were fantasy became too real. *The devil takes a woman's body to perpetuate his work. The devil is possessed to seize a virgin for his mistress.* This strange woman was the devil, surely, taking himself a virgin mistress.

Squire Richmond was not a man of courage, but he lunged forward, his hands outstretched, toward Martha's throat. Abigail seized both his hands, and held them firm.

"You will not harm her," Abigail spat out her words, and Squire felt the vicious force behind them.

"I love you, Abigail."

"If you harm her, you harm me. To kill her is to murder me."

Squire let his fists drop to his side. He didn't know the devil's rules, he hadn't listened hard in the church school, and he saw now why his inattentiveness dismayed his father. A knowledge of God was necessary; it taught a man to fight the devil. Perhaps Abigail would die if he killed the devil while she was still in his possession. He backed away. There were wise men, like his father, who were prepared to exorcise such devils.

"Goodbye, Squire Richmond." The sound of Abigail's sweet voice replayed in his head as Squire ran hard down the hillside, mounted his horse, and, breathless, rode to find his father in the village square.

Red stopped short in the doorway of his cabin, out of breath, and leaned against the doorframe, his hand across his eyes. He knew quite clearly where he'd been and what he'd seen there in the woods, but he understood none of it. He rubbed his forehead and tried to remember if he'd

112

found the lost girl, but all he saw before him were the naked women, Cynthia and Angela, in the act of making love.

"Mommy!"

Cynthia and Angela were dressed. They stood, hand in hand, between the oaks, as though they had been frozen there in time.

"Mommy!" Janet pushed through blackberries, and heard a snake slide quickly from her footsteps.

"Mommy!"

"Janet!" Cynthia ran toward the bushes and, reaching in among the brambles, lifted her daughter to safe ground. "Where have you been, honey? Mommy's been so worried."

Cynthia squatted and held the girl tight. Janet smiled into her mother's shoulder, hoping the moment would never end.

"I got lost," she said, and clung, her arms tight about Cynthia's neck, as she was carried through the dark woods to the old house.

Cynthia bathed the girl herself, and fed her, leading her then to bed and holding her until she fell asleep. Even when Janet's breaths were slow and deep, Cynthia still sat on the bed beside her, reluctant to return downstairs, reluctant to come face to face with Angela.

When Angela had bedded Pete down for the night, she sat on the front porch alone and listened to the rustle of the little creatures foraging in the woods beyond. She longed for Cynthia, as Abigail had longed for Martha, and she was ready to face any unknown danger to prolong that love.

It was nearly eight when Cynthia walked out onto the porch. She looked at Angela but didn't smile. She stared through the dark mesh screen beyond the hilltop, toward the darkened world that slept out of her sight. At last, she turned and sat by Angela on the lounge chair.

It was a settee, designed to seat two, built on metal rods and springs so that it would rock. It rocked now, making rusty creaking sounds against the silent night, the slight movement of the women's rigid, motionless bodies causing the cushions to sigh and wheeze.

Angela, so nervous that her head jerked when she turned, glanced at Cynthia. Cynthia continued to stare ahead. Angela listened to the rhythm of their breathing, in perfect tandem, and, with fear, laid her hand open on the space between them. She didn't see Cynthia look at her or at her hand, but, moments later, Cynthia's fingers gently found her palm and stroked it, then entwined their fingers firmly.

"I love you." Angela whispered.

Cynthia listened hard to the three words; she replayed them several times inside her head, until she was certain it was not Abigail, but Angela, who spoke.

"No," Cynthia said softly, "it's not our love, it's theirs."

"I think I loved you before them. I think I loved you the first time that I saw you, pulling Pete's stroller up to the stairway in the apartment building."

"Don't, Angela."

"I might never have said that to you. I might never have let you know. Abigail has taught me to be brave." Angela laughed gently, nervously, and tightened her hand around Cynthia's, feeling damp perspiration grow between their palms.

"You're young," Cynthia said, tonelessly, "and impressionable. It's just that Abigail feels so strongly you feel it, too, and believe it's you. I have the same reaction. I seem to take on Martha's feelings, even when she's gone."

Angela caught her breath; she clung tightly to Cynthia's hands and hoped her fingers didn't tremble. She could hardly speak. "You mean you love me?"

"We're possessed, Angela. Bizarre as it seems, we *are* possessed. Almost nothing that we feel or do now comes from us. We're feeling their feelings, we're living out their story." Cynthia said coldly, academically.

Angela spoke softly, as though she hadn't heard. "I always knew that when I fell in love, it would be with a woman. Other girls in school had fantasies about boys like the football captain, but mine were centered on women, usually teachers." The dry night air stirred. "My friends dreamed of being rescued by some handsome, muscular movie star, ripped from the clutches of death by some all-powerful man who would take them home and worship at

114

their feet." She laughed tentatively and glanced at Cynthia, but Cynthia's eyes were focused out beyond the screen again. "I think they're mostly married, pregnant and living in the Bronx now." Cynthia laughed, low, but she didn't turn to meet Angela's anxious look. "I dreamed about a woman who would hold me close, who would need me. It was as though I had to find the other half of me."

"I felt that, for my mother," Cynthia admitted softly, "I felt it took the two of us to face the world. Without the sex, of course." She cleared her throat quickly, and forced a laugh. "I never felt about a woman, though, the way that Martha feels for Abigail."

Angela closed her eyes tightly, as though not seeing could erase what she'd heard.

"Dave will be here Friday," Cynthia continued, "we only have one day left. I want it to be finished by then, Angela."

It took every bit of Angela's courage to speak. "Kiss me."

"No." But Cynthia turned toward her.

"Kiss me." It was an order this time. "Kiss me. I know you want to."

"I can't." Cynthia's lower lip was trembling. "I can't do it, Angela. We're not Martha and Abigail, needing one another to fight against the world. I have a husband and two children; you have your whole life in front of you."

"I love you." The order became a plea. Cynthia stroked Angela's dark hair as though she were comforting a child. The night was still and dark around them, only the occasional fiddle of a cricket filtered through the screen. They sat that way a long time, Cynthia's stroking Angela's thick hair with one hand, the other entwined tightly with Angela's. Angela leaned back and to the side, dropping her head on Cynthia's upper arm. A moment passed before she felt Cynthia's fingers leave her hair and find the blushing flesh of her cheek, turning her head until their lips met.

"I shouldn't do this," but as she said the words, Cynthia's other hand was leaving Angela's to cross her lap and pull their bodies close together. The passion and the need grew quickly strong and Angela and Cynthia made love for the first time, knowing somehow as they did so that it was the last for Abigail and Martha.

Chapter Eleven

As rigid as a corpse, Red Richmond lay on the bed in his small cabin. He couldn't sleep, he was waiting for something and he was rigid with the fear of it. He hadn't gone up to the house tonight, not after what he'd seen between the women in the woods. He was embarrassed for them, embarrassed for himself and totally bewildered by the fantastic story that kept replaying like an endless reel in his mind. He wondered if he'd seen a film like this at some time, or read a book, its story hidden in the deep recesses of his subconscious. Perhaps he was going mad; his mother had a mad uncle, there was madness in the family. He sweated in the humid cabin, holding the August afternoon heat, and waited for something.

It came, at last, and Red gave himself fully to it. He never left the bed inside his cabin, he never moved or cried out, he didn't speak aloud the strange sentences, as he had done before. He lay rigid, pooled in sweat, and watched himself, as young Squire Richmond.

Squire's fury mounted as he rode into the village; he found his father quickly. In ugly words, red-faced, he spat out the scene he'd witnessed on the hill. The blood drained from his father's face, and Squire knew then that his father had not believed in witches till this moment. Although he'd ordered five women burned in the past year, he believed only in human demons and discounted such intangibles as God and the Devil. Squire's gift for words embroidered on the story; Martha's fierce, devilish appearance became the awesome figure of Lucifer, bent on destroying mankind.

By the time Squire had repeated his story for the council, he'd added, in the manner of good balladeers, a forked tail, cloven feet, and eyes that shot out yellow sparks. The council members sat, some with their mouths half open, some with their hands and legs trembling beneath the table. The villagers who circled the open council, and watched its nightly meetings, moaned low, wives buried their heads in their husbands' shoulders, and children wrapped their mothers' skirts around them, putting their fingers to their ears. The more Squire elaborated on his story, the more he heard waves of horror gasp and moan among his audience, the more true and vivid it all became to him.

At the moment when the council members rose to their feet, as one man, and lifted up their fists to signify AYE!, Squire would have sworn at the Holy Gates that every word he'd spoken was perfect truth.

They rode hard to the hill, two dozen of the strongest village men, armed with knives and muskets and praying loudly to God, calling on His assistance, in case He was occupied with lesser matters and failed to notice the bravery that they were showing in His name.

To a man, they were belly-hard with terror, but faith and courage boiled in their blood, and when the horses rode roughly enough and their joined voices were loud enough, they felt bonded in righteousness, as men do when they fly into the face of battle, certain that they will die with honor.

Martha and Abigail lay beyond the cabin, naked, making love as though they knew it was the last time. Jeremiah, sleeping soundly inside, turned over to drape a loving arm around his yellow dog. He dreamed of throwing sticks for his new playmate. *"Fetch, boy, fetch,"* he was saying in his dreams.

The intensity between the women mounted, although they could not hear the men dismount at the foot of the hill and move silently through the dark forest, upward, toward them.

"I cannot love you hard enough, deep enough," Martha whispered, and Abigail, beneath her, pressed upward, opening herself to Martha's hand. *"This body of mine is not poet enough to show you all my love."*

"I wish that I could open like a cloak and take all of you inside of me and we'd be one, forever."

"It can't be so, my Abby. You are you and I am I. Only our love will join us, forever."

"It is vast, this love. So great that sometimes I can scarcely bear it."

"Woman's love, unleashed, is too great a force for men to reckon with, my mother told me once."

"Like God, it frightens them." Abigail laughed softly, her lips moving at Martha's throbbing temple.

"Hush, Abby. Let me love you."

And they brought each other to a moment of completion so filled with life it might have been the moment of their birth, painful, sobbing, breaking free together in a world unknown.

The dog barked first.

Alarmed, the women sat up, scrambling for their clothing, but it was too late. In a shaft of moonlight, they watched the yellow mongrel hunch and bare his fangs at the mass of black-cloaked figures, who now broke through the clearing and spread out, circling the cabin.

"They're over here, I've found them!"

The scattered figures drew together in a mob and swarmed on Martha and Abigail. The yellow dog howled, flew into the midst and tore the flesh of the Elder Richmond's buttocks.

"The dog is the devil's, too," the Elder Richmond shouted, "it is known the devil takes the soul of a dumb creature to accompany him!"

The Elder Richmond grasped the dog's hind legs. Before the cur could turn and bite, the eldest Richmond son had clasped its muzzle and its crown, and, in a single motion, snapped its neck.

"She is the devil, sure," Zeke Horton, young and tough and Godly, seized Martha by the shoulders and held her up to the torchlight. She tried to cover up her nakedness but Zeke's boy, Rodman, eleven and sturdy for his age, held down her hands.

In the torchlight, Martha's long blonde hair, tangled and wild about her head, glinted, seemed to sparkle, and her blue eyes, with the flame held at her face, reflected yellow.

The men gasped.

Abigail tore at Zeke Horton with her fingernails, but

118

Squire Richmond grasped her, and held her tightly, his fingers digging into the soft flesh of her breasts.

"I'm going to free you, Abigail," he promised, his words hot and moist against her ear, *"I am going to save your soul."*

"My soul is mine," she hissed; she dug at his hands with her nails until she drew blood, and she spat into his face, *"I shall do with my soul as I please."*

"God wants you saved." Squire Richmond, caught up in the greatness of the moment and overwhelmed by Angela's naked body in his arms, felt no pain from the scratches.

"Damn God!"

The men stopped, gasped, and stared at Abigail through the torch-light.

"She is possessed, no doubt of it," The Elder Richmond pronounced, and the rumble from the men became a cheer. They all focused then on Martha, the devil they were charged to exorcise.

"We are righteous men," the Elder Richmond said, above the bloody shout, *"and we will try this devil fairly, as is God's will."*

There were four men who lifted Martha, naked, on their shoulders. Four others walked beside them, and held her limbs from fighting, kicking.

"Mother!"

They had nearly left the clearing when the boy called out. Dressed in a skirt, he ran stumbling after them, his face streaked and grubby, dragging the dead yellow cur.

"Progeny of the devil!"

Zeke Horton's boy hid behind his father, and a man named Matthew Lucas grabbed Jeremiah, ripping the dead dog from the child's hand. He slung the boy like a flour sack across his shoulder.

"God's will be done, God's will be done, God's will be done," they chanted as they marched the path down the long hillside. The birds were still, the crickets ceased their sound, and the stars, it seemed to Martha, held aloft above the men, dimmed their light.

Squire Richmond had to seek help in holding Abigail as they walked. She struggled wildly and succeeded once in seizing Martha's finger, holding so tightly to it that Martha felt the nail loosen as they ripped Abby's grasp away.

"*I love you, Martha*," Abby repeated, shouting, until Squire Richmond tore his kerchief from his neck and jammed it deep into her mouth.

"*Mother!*" The boy screamed, then Matthew Lucas hit him hard across the face and he gave up the fight, passive and weeping on the big man's shoulder.

Martha, naked, held helpless and staring at the unblinking stars, opened her mouth but could not speak. Inside, she heard the words she'd said before to Abby.

She that liveth in pleasure is dead while she liveth . . . Sit still, my daughter, until thou know how the matter will fall: for the man will not be in rest, until he have finished the thing this day . . .

She pressed her lips against her teeth, trying to provide the wetness that would allow her to speak. At last, she forced them, rasping, from her throat. "*I love you, Abigail.*"

She felt the blow across her eyes, a filling in her nostril and the thick slow trickle of blood that ran across her lips, into her mouth, wet and salty on her tongue. It enabled her to speak again.

"*It is too great, too great for men to reckon with.*"

A blow came again, against her mouth this time. She felt the sharp smack, nothing, then the parting of the flesh above her lip. The blood ran fast; she had to turn her head and spit it out to keep from smothering in it. She screamed once, then fell silent.

At the foot of the hill, the cart sat, tipped backwards, unhitched, waiting for its cargo. Martha was loaded on it, standing, her naked arms and legs tied to its side railings. Her breasts and belly, dark with blood, were hardly visible in the dark night.

Squire hoisted Abigail onto his horse and mounted up behind her, covering her nakedness with his cloak, but keeping one hand underneath it, holding her, digging his fingers deep enough into her breast so that her nipple, rigid with the chill of fear, pierced hard into his palm. His mind was hot with anger and revenge, his body charged with the

120

male excitement of the hunt, his genitals reared and ready, pressing hard against Abigail's bare buttocks.

The boy was held, too, on a horse, but he rode backwards, burying his terrified and streaked face in Matthew Lucas's sweat-stained weskit. He clung to the man's damp clothing as though it were his line to life, and he prayed wordlessly that his mother wouldn't cry aloud again.

Chapter Twelve

Martha could scarcely keep her footing on the cart, hitched and under way, hurtling along the rutted dirt road toward the village. The cart crashed and swayed from side to side, slamming her against the railings, tearing her flesh with the ragged hemp ropes that held her. Her feet would leave the floorboards, and her body lurch forward, then jerked back by the tautness of her bonds, she'd regain her balance only to fall again. She flailed but did not struggle with the bonds; it took all her effort to remain conscious, thrashed wildly as she was by the forward movement of the cart.

When the cart rolled to a stop and threw her backwards on the railing, splinters sliding underneath the skin across her back, she wept with relief. She hung, squatting, her weight supported by the bonds around her wrists, until the Elder Richmond cut the rope. Then she was carried by the same four men into the chancel of the wooden church.

A cloak was pressed around her, its thick wool sticking in the wet blood on her body.

"She must be covered so that women, too, may watch. It is their souls at stake here, every one."

The room was filled with benches and sapling chairs, each occupied by fierce, wide-eyed men, leaning forward, their knees on their elbows, to see and hear better. Between them, around them, and circling the room, their women stood, their faces half hidden behind the safety of their cloaks. At the windows, children's faces pressed, noses and mouths distorted, eyes wide with new excitement.

In the cloakroom beside the church, Abigail was fitted with a dress by a stout woman, dedicated to the service of the clergy.

"This is my girl's dress and we can ill afford to give it up."

Abigail pushed at the woman's fingers, and the sleeve of the garment parted at the seam.

"There's no wearing dresses once the devil's used them. I'll be charged to burn it now, you know."

It took the woman and Squire Richmond a quarter of an hour to force Abigail, resisting, into the dress. One sleeve was torn out in the struggle, and the bodice seam was ripped open from the arm to the waist; still she was covered well enough for women's eyes.

They took her in and bound her to a chair, Squire holding her as the stout woman tied the cords in the intricate small knots she used for crewel work.

Jeremiah sat in Matthew Lucas' lap, his head turned into Matthew's sour smelling shirt, his eyes closed tightly, trying not to hear or see. He wadded Matthew's weskit in his fists and held on tight. Between his clenched small fingers, yellow sprigs of the dog's hair jutted out, stuck in sweat and trembling with each exhale of Matthew's breath.

Martha, swaddled in the heavy cloak, was lashed to the centerpole which stood erect, dead-center, in the church. Around her, she could hear murmuring, a hushed and ominous sound like wild weeds in a field before a storm. Her mouth was dry, her lip broken and scabbing over. It was beyond her to speak.

The gavel came down hard on the pine pulpit. The Elder Richmond stood, his face placid, his eyes seeming to look beyond the room.

His voice was slow and toneless. *"This woman, known as Martha, is accused of witchery by young Squire Richmond, a respected and godly resident of this village. Come forward, Squire, and make your public testimony."*

The excitement of the hunt was past, the candle-lit reality of life and death was on him and Squire Richmond shook as he stood. He felt Abigail's look, dark and rich with hate, cold against his left cheek as he moved through the seated villagers, and pressed around their women, to reach the pulpit. His father sat down, leaving the pulpit empty. Squire had no choice but to stand behind it.

"There," he said, his voice quiet and trembling, *"sits Abi-*

gail, my father's tenant farmer's daughter, orphaned this year." He could feel the drama that his words created, the strain of the villagers to hear his every word. *"She was a fine girl, handy in the home and helpful in the farming, a just and godly girl."*

An old man coughed, and several villagers adjusted themselves on creaking chairs.

"Louder!"

"Abigail," Squire forced his voice, and motioned to her stoic figure, bound to the sapling chair, *"was a fine and godly girl."*

The old man coughed again, and said *"Ahem."*

Squire fished frantically inside his mind for words. He could not, for a moment, recall why he was there. The faces blurred and the coughing increased, peppering the silence of the room.

"Go on, son."

It was his father's voice, filled for the first time in Squire's life with love and pride. Squire cleared his throat again and squared his shoulders. His knees weak and his voice trembling, he spoke.

"She has my love, this orphan girl, and with the approval of my father, I rode out to the hill today to find her and ask her to be my wife."

Murmuring broke out, intensified, then dwindled. It was clear that the men viewed this with suspicion, but the romantic aspect of a rich young man in love with an orphaned girl was favored by the women.

"It was there that I found her, naked, in an embrace with the devil who is lashed here in our midst."

The faces in the room turned all at once to Martha; she closed her eyes, but she could feel their stares invading and penetrating her, still naked underneath the cloak. The crowd shuddered as they looked at Martha, sweat and blood-stained, black from being dragged through dirt, her blonde hair wild and studded with burrs and briars from the struggle. Those standing nearest her moved quickly, those sitting scraped their chairs across the wooden floor, to put space between themselves and her.

Squire continued, *"The devil . . ."*

The Elder Richmond placed his hand on his son's arm.

"You can't call her a devil until we've proved her one; that is the law." He said it softly, out of the villager's hearing.

"The woman," Squire began again and flushed with his lack of legal knowledge, *"the woman, Martha, she calls herself, spoke to me, and claimed that she was married to my Abigail, that she herself was clergy, and that the God she served lived with her in the woods."*

There was a sharp intake of breath throughout the room, and mutterings of *"Witch!"* became loud cries.

The Elder Richmond stood and hushed them with his hand. *"We are God's people and we give fair trial, even to the devil."*

A low muttering continued, but Squire Richmond went on, his voice rising with emotion. *"I asked her to come with me and marry me, my Abigail, and she spoke the same words as the devil's. And when I reached to strangle the life out of the witch woman, Abigail informed me that, if I killed the devil, she too would die."*

The men sat upright in their chairs, and women huddled to the wall. Outside the window, the children's faces disappeared; they ran for safety.

"I could not kill the woman I most loved, and I knew surely that God would pardon me for allowing this witch-woman to continue living until I sought help in the village from wiser men than I." Squire swallowed hard, wishing he could say he'd destroyed the devil by himself and wondering if his reluctance to kill the woman he loved was an unmanly thing.

"You might have lost your soul, Squire," Matthew called out loudly in support, his heaving chest rocking Jeremiah's body as he spoke, *"No one man's strong enough to take the devil by himself."*

A murmured AYE! went through the crowd.

"I believe," Squire continued, bouyed by the male support, *"the woman Martha to be a witch, possessed by Lucifer, and to have taken the virgin soul of Abigail to bride."* A moan chorused within the church. *"I believe that if, in God's name, we destroy the witch, the devil will depart and leave my Abigail's soul in the state of godly goodness in which it was born."* A muttering of AYES! threatened to

rise again. Squire added quickly. *"That is my public testimony, the truth as I saw it, God be my judge."*

"God's will be done," the crowd shouted in response. It was good testimony, and the men smiled openly; the women smiled, perhaps, too, hidden by their cloaks.

"She must pass the tests," the Elder Richmond said then; he approached Martha at the centerpole. *"Woman, avert your eyes, please. It is necessary that this thing be done."*

The Elder Richmond removed his tie pin, three inches long and rusty.

"A true witch, possessed by the devil, has a place on her body where she feels no pain."

He plunged the tie pin into Martha's forearm and, drymouthed, she moaned. Blood appeared when the pin was withdrawn. Again; into her thigh, and then her calves, her belly and her breast. Each time she cried out hoarsely, protesting pain. At last he thrust the pin into her cheek, the same cheek that had been beaten twice as she was carried down the hill. She felt the entrance of the spike; she felt it sink through the flesh and pierce her dry, numbed tongue. There was no pain.

"Witch!"

Women peeked from underneath their cloaks to see the point of witchery; they winced against the sinfulness of Martha's body, filthy, bruised and naked.

"Examine her," Matthew Lucas demanded, *"Examine her for devil's herbs. If she is burned with the devil's medicine on her, we'll take in the fumes and lose our souls!"*

The Elder Richmond lifted Martha's breasts and felt beneath them. He dug his fingers into her armpits, scraped his nails behind her ears.

"Cut her hair," Matthew Lucas cried out, *"it may be hidden in her hair!"*

Squire Richmond, bouyed by success, withdrew his hunting knife, and, grabbing Martha's hair in full handfuls, severed it in clumps until the Elder Richmond could examine all her scalp with his long nails.

Abigail could not see what was happening to Martha. The standing, gaping men blocked Abby's view. She gagged against the handkerchief, dry and aching in her mouth, and swallowed back the vomit that rose up to her throat with every breath.

The Elder Richmond knelt; all the men's heads moved forward. They squatted, some of them, or knelt, or sat, to watch.

He put his whole hand in her at once, jamming and forcing entry, tearing tissues and flesh until his fingers touched her cervix and scraped the entire channel. He satisfied himself it hid no herbs. Her moan was something beyond human, a terrifying death knell of the soul. With his fist inside her, she felt the tightness in her belly turn loose. Her menses flowed; her thighs were red with blood and shame.

They carried her to the Square, for she could no longer walk, and they lashed her upright to the stake.

The Elder Richmond was now convinced that the woman was a witch, possessed by the devil. Satan had made a home on Richmond Hill; that thought sent a wave of fear through the Elder Richmond. Perhaps it was a penance, God's warning to him. Perhaps God knew that Elder Richmond had deserted a mistress and a bastard daughter on that hill; perhaps God knew that the child came to the Elder Richmond, a decade later, and begged help for her dying mother. There'd been choice but to refuse the girl; a young man seeking to be the Elder of a village could not admit he'd sired a bastard. He knew the woman and the child could not have survived that bitter winter.

He watched the men pull the knots tight around the witch's arms. *Oh God,* the Elder Richmond prayed silently for the first time in his life, *I yielded to the temptations of lust and failed You. Now You have faced me with the devil. I will not fail You this time.*

He spoke aloud to Martha. "If you have last words, you may say them now."

Martha's tongue was too hideously swollen. No limb still bore human feelings. Her head hung from her shoulders, a lifeless, heavy weight.

She saw the man she believed to be her father stoop, strike a match and set the kindling at her feet. She saw the stiff-backed young man she believed to be half-brother to her tighten his grip on Abigail's arms. As the kindling smouldered and smoke drifted upwards, she saw Abigail close her eyes and press her face into Squire's jacket. Martha let her eyelids close, too, and she did not see Matthew Lucas raise Jeremiah high into the air.

"Look, boy. Watch the witch burn. Learn your lesson."

The flames enveloped her legs first, then caught and flared the hemline of the cloak. The pain was beyond bearing. Martha, the face of Abigail etched on her mind and heart, the remembered smell of Abigail's sweet skin blotting out the acrid smoke, lost consciousness, echoing a dirge inside her.

God's will be done.

Martha was gone before the flames enveloped her. Squire urged Abigail to watch.

"When this is done, you'll belong to me."

At the end, they doused the flames with water, and the village cheered.

"The witch is burned, boy," Matthew said to Jeremiah, atop his shoulders, *"Cheer, boy, cheer, God is victorious!"*

And Jeremiah, his tears dried from the blistering heat that enveloped the village square, emotion fear-frozen in his belly, cheered as loud as any other boy, the yellow dog hair still stuck to his waving fingers.

When Squire at last removed the kerchief from Abigail's mouth, she lurched forward, spilling vomit on the earth. The stout church woman brought her water.

Squire smiled down at her as the woman picked loose her bonds.

"It is done," Squire said proudly, and took her hand.

She whispered, *"The Lord do so to me, and more also, if ought but death part thee and me . . . Martha, my love, forgive me."*

"What?"

Squire leaned forward to hear better.

"Nothing."

Abigail looked up at him but she could not meet his eyes, ever again.

Angela and Cynthia lay together on the lounge chair, holding each other, weeping silently.

Chapter Thirteen

When the possession ended, Red found himself standing outside his father's cabin. His hands were on his hips, his feet placed firmly and protectively on the path that led up to the old house. He was staring toward the village as though the smoke from Martha's burning might still be curling in the night sky. He broke the stance and rubbed his eyes. He was disoriented by the dark and it took a moment for him to get his bearings. Then, he broke into a sweat and began to run.

The women made no motion to sit up, receive him, when Red's steps broke the silence. He came in the porch door, saw the women interlocked in grief as he knew they would be, and sat beside them in a wooden rocking chair.

They knew where they had been that night, all three of them, and they sat silently, looking beyond the porch to the same ancient stand of pines that had, three hundred years before, witnessed the horror on this hill.

Their vigil was interrupted by Pete's terrified scream from the upstairs bedroom.

The scream seemed unceasing, but Cynthia moved slowly, knowing she couldn't abate the boy's fright. He had to live it as they had, he had to let the horror burst forth fully into life so it, at last, could die. Untangling herself from Angela's tight grasp, Cynthia stood and straightened her blouse, smoothed her slacks, slipped her rubber sandals on her feet. She moved forward with effort, as though the air around her, thick with time, still wished to hold her back.

She took the sleeping boy in her arms and rocked him till he woke and the screaming stopped, unleashing racking wails and tears.

"It was a nightmare, honey, don't be frightened."

"Mommy!"

"Don't be frightened, Pete; it was a dream. It's over now."

Janet, who'd been awakened by the cries, stood trembling in the hallway, peering into the room, tore between the terror of his screams and jealousy that, once again, he was in the favored place, in their mother's arms.

On the porch, Angela straightened her clothing and sat upright on the lounge chair. Red fumbled in his pocket and lit a cigarette, loosing a stream of smoke. "I'm sorry." He reached across the armrest of the lounge chair and touched her hand.

His words, soft as his touch, burned into Angela's ears and skin. She pulled her hand from him and swallowed hard.

"It wasn't us, you know," he said.

She couldn't look at him. She stared beyond the porch.

"I wonder if it ever really happened." He spoke again.

A rock of grief was wedged in Angela's throat. She couldn't speak.

"You know," Red continued, his voice low, respectful, "psychologists say that some people can dream the same dreams at the same time. They've tested it; it's true. One person can have a dream so strongly that it invades the subconscious of people nearby. It's a form of ESP."

Angela still sat silently, as though she didn't hear him. In the brush, below the porch, a small creature skittered through leaves.

"Of course," Red continued, "there are people who actually believe in ghosts. A couple of universities sponsor research in that kind of thing."

Angela placed her elbows on her knees and lowered her face into her hands.

"When I lived in the commune, we had seances." Red injected a tentative note of levity into his voice. "I used to move the table with my knee and this girl, Joan, would get all wild-eyed and holler, 'Here comes the spirit!'" He laughed softly. "She got me back, though. She read my Tarot cards and said I should walk carefully through life.

That afternoon I stepped on a cotton-mouth; bit the shit out of me, I had to go to the emergency ward."

Angela wanted to cry. There was a great well in her, pushing at her ribcage, but it was dammed up. Her eyes were red and dry.

Red had been no less affected than the women by what had happened to them all, but he had no way of showing it. To weep, to express his confusion and fear, would seem unmanly. Alone, he'd do just that, but here, two shaken women had no man but him to depend on. He felt that his presence, while annoying to Angela at the moment, was necessary. He wished he knew what words would comfort her. He wanted to ease the terrible tension between them. Nothing that he said seemed right.

"Cynthia's husband gets here tomorrow, huh?"

Angela forced herself to nod, mentally manipulating the muscles of her neck as if she were a puppeteer.

"You suppose the boy's all right?"

She couldn't nod again.

"He's stopped crying, anyway."

She turned her back to him.

Red was strangely grateful that this terrifying night had happened to them both. They'd shared an experience of magnitude. Squire Richmond's love for Abigail had brought Red closer to Angela, had seemed to make them intimate before the fact. Red knew, however, that Angela bore the residual hate and distrust of him that Abigail had felt, and with good cause, for Squire. Red knew he had to win her trust to win her heart.

"What can I do, Angela? I want to help."

She sat motionless, her face again buried in her hands, and didn't answer.

Red resisted his instinct to embrace her, hold her close. He glanced down at his watch. Ten forty-five. He sat beside her, quietly, motionless, hoping that his presence would make her feel secure.

Cynthia was tired to the bone. She hardly had the strength to move from Pete's room to her own. She fell across the bed, too exhausted to remove her clothes. As she lay there, staring at the long, thin cracks across the plaster ceiling, she felt a slipperiness between her legs. Her period. She tried vainly to remember if it was her time. Perhaps, she thought wearily, it wasn't her period, but Martha's. It was too confusing; she turned her face into the pillow and blotted out all thought.

Angela pulled herself upstairs by holding onto the bannister. On the second floor, she leaned against the wall; the porous wallpaper absorbed perspiration from her forehead.

She might have turned right, a few steps into her own room, to fall onto her own bed. Instead she moved along the hallway, forcing herself to walk, until she reached the door to Cynthia's room. She stood in the doorway, her weight against the doorframe, and looked at Cynthia lying there, arms and legs akimbo, a rag doll idly tossed onto the bed.

Cynthia sensed Angela's presence and turned her head slowly, not lifting it, to look at Angela. Moments passed. Outside, a branch, caught by a gust of night wind, brushed the windowpane. They looked at one another until the intensity between them became a path that must be traveled. Cynthia lifted her arm and held her hand out to Angela.

Angela moved slowly toward the bed and lay beside her, her head on Cynthia's shoulder, Cynthia's arm folded around Angela's neck. Angela felt the rising and falling of Cynthia's breast and the movement made her groggy. She closed her eyes.

"It's over," Cynthia said softly.

"I don't think so," Angela replied.

Cynthia's mouth was thick and feverish with lack of sleep, with sheer exhaustion, but she turned her face to Angela and kissed the girl's closed eyelids.

"Oh, God," Cynthia said, finally, "I hope it's over."

Angela lay staring at the ceiling. "Their love was strong enough to last beyond their death."

"Nearly three hundred years."

"I love you, Cynthia."

Cynthia turned her face from Angela's. "No," she said firmly, "No. It's over. Go to bed now, Angela, get some sleep. You'll feel differently tomorrow morning."

Angela didn't go to her room, though her body cried for rest. She walked to the front porch and stood looking down the hill—toward Abigail's first home, toward the village where Abigail last saw Martha.

"Are you all right?" Red stood, then walked across the porch until he was beside her. He touched her arm.

She didn't pull away. She needed the comfort of a loving hand. Abandoned now by Abigail and Martha, rejected by Cynthia, Angela felt desperately alone.

"You ought to get some sleep." Red hugged her shoulders.

"I can't sleep." She felt his warm breath against her hair.

"You need to get out of this house, then. Come on. I'll make a pot of coffee." He engulfed her hand in his and led her down the porch steps toward his cabin. She thought, at first, that Red was right. She thought that putting distance between herself and the distraught spirits of Abigail and Martha might reassure her. By the time they reached Red's cabin, she knew that she was wrong. It wasn't over, yet. Something terrifying still hung in the air and Angela clung to the fabric of Red's sleeve for reassurance.

Although Cynthia kept her eyes closed, sleep wouldn't come. She felt sticky, soiled. Perspiration, sleep and menstrual blood mingled on her body. She stood up suddenly, snatched the stained sheets and mattress cover from the bed and hurried down the hallway to the bathroom. She stripped off her clothing and shoved it, with the sheets and cover, into the hamper. She adjusted the faucets of the shower until the water ran lukewarm, then stepped into it gratefully. The pool around her feet was dark, then pink, then clear; she worked the soap into a lather and scrubbed her body thoroughly. She washed her scalp so fiercely that it tingled. Finally, the water at her feet was sudless, pure.

She had dried herself, found a tampon and was pulling her robe tightly around herself when the bathroom door flew open.

"I gotta pee-pee." Pete staggered sleepily toward the toilet.

"I told you to knock before you come into the bathroom," Cynthia snapped. A part of her, however, was relieved. At least he hadn't wet the bed.

Pete watched the stream of urine that shot out of his small penis. He proudly looked up at his mother.

"Watch what you're doing," she said sharply, "you'll miss the bowl."

He did, and his mother wiped it up with paper towel. Boys were better, Pete knew that. Nobody had to tell him; he could see it for himself. All the important people in the world were male, except mothers. Last year, he thought he'd like to be a mother someday but everybody in nursery school laughed at him. If Janet pee-peed on the floor, his mother would have a fit. He stood, cradling his penis in his hand, and watched his mother wiping up the puddle. She didn't even scold him. He wanted to ask his mother if he could sleep in her bed. He was still frightened by the terrible dream he'd had; somebody had killed his yellow dog and he couldn't find his mother. If Janet found out that he'd asked to sleep in their mother's bed, she'd call him a scairdy-cat. Bravely, Pete walked back to his room and curled beneath the covers in a fetal position. He repeated his mother's words, "It's only a dream, it's over now," until he fell asleep again.

Cynthia returned to her room and lay on the bed. Pete was dependent on her. Dave was dependent on her, too. She had encouraged their dependence, gotten a sense of power from it. Now, it irritated her.

Sleep still evaded her. Let go, she told herself, let go. She tried to relax one muscle at a time, but even though her body relaxed, became dead weight against the mattress, her mind would not rest.

She tried to picture living with a woman. Angela across the breakfast table, instead of Dave. She thought of growing old beside a woman, two baskets of needlepoint beside the rocking chairs.

She envisioned Dave's face if she told him she was leaving him to love a woman. He wouldn't take it seriously. She'd heard him speak of homosexual couples before. "They're playing house, it isn't real."

She thought of Martha and Abigail and knew that Dave was wrong.

It was academic, anyway, she told herself; she wasn't in love with Angela. But if she were—Cynthia'd lived through Martha's love for Abigail and understood its beauty and its strength.

Cynthia wondered if Angela would ever love a man. It didn't matter. No one was hunting witches, anymore. No one evoked the name of God to persecute people different than themselves. No sane person believed that homosexuality was a contagious disease.

However Angela might live her life, Cynthia assured herself as she drifted into sleep, she'd never face the danger that destroyed Martha and Abigail. Squire Richmond had been dead three hundred years.

"Here it is," Red said and pulled a dusty ledger from the top shelf on his bookcase. "I knew it was here somewhere. My mother used to be a real bug on family history." He blew the cobwebs off the crumbling cover of the book and backed down the stepladder.

He approached Angela cautiously. She'd hardly said a word in the half hour that she'd been there. He told himself that she was still in shock. They'd shared a terrifying experience.

"These are the original land transactions." He opened the book and spread it on her lap. He was pleased to see her look down at the faded writing, interest on her face.

"Here," she said, and pointed her finger at the second entry on the page.

The parcel known as Richmond Hill—to Squire and Abigail Richmond, a wedding gift, 18th August, 1691, transferred from the parcel known as Richmond land by Mathias Richmond, Village Elder, rightful and deeded owner.

"Today's the 5th," Angela whispered, staring at the entry.

"She married him soon afterward, I guess." Red studied the other transactions and moved close to Angela.

"She had no choice." Angela leaned away from him and looked out the window. A cedar tree, outlined against the sky, swayed gently back and forth. It looked so lonely. Angela felt tears spill from her eyes again and she wiped them with her fingers.

Red knew he was losing her attention. He patted her knee. "And look at this." He underscored the entry with his finger.

The parcel known as Richmond Hill—to Jeremiah Richmond, Village Clergy, by his mother, Abigail Richmond, deceased 11th February, 1705.

"Clergy." Angela shook her head as though she couldn't believe the word. "Jeremiah became a minister."

"But Abby wasn't Jeremiah's mother." Red paged further through the book.

"She would have taken him in, though. She would have raised him for Martha."

"I don't see anymore about Squire. Abby must have outlived him."

"She lived just long enough to raise the boy." Angela closed the covers of the book and laid it on the floor.

"It wasn't a dream, then." Red put his arm around Angela's shoulders.

"I never thought it was."

"Well, it's over now." Red gently pulled Angela to her feet and held her close against him.

Angela knew it wasn't over and, frightened, she welcomed Red's embrace.

He didn't rush her. He was not a zealous, selfish lover. He cared deeply for her and when he realized that she was a virgin, he felt a sense of responsibilty which seemed to strengthen him, allowing him to kiss her gently, whisper to her, stroke her body softly through her clothing, until he'd won her trust enough to lead her to the bed.

She showed no signs of arousal. Though Red held her tenderly, locked his tongue with hers, and moved his fingers on the places which should have caused her to moan with longing, she lay passive in the circle of his arms.

"I want you to want me, too," he whispered, his lips brushing her ear. "I want it to be good for you."

Angela felt nothing except the slight discomfort of his weight on her. She tried to recreate the deep wanting she'd felt with Cynthia, the trembling, crying need to become one with another person. But Red was male, all male. He felt and smelled male, hard and muscular, heavy against her thighs. She knew that he was holding back his own need, trying to please her. But, try as she might, she felt no flicker of desire.

Red was aware that she was dry, unexcited. He would not enter her that way, he would not force and hurt her.

"Want me," he begged, and he used his mouth to love her, "Want me, Angela, want me the way I want you."

They worked at it. He loving her, she trying to please him, and to prove to herself that she could love a man. At last, she couldn't bear the writhing of his body over her any longer; she pushed at him and he moved away.

"I can't," she said and sat up on the bed.

Red lay on his back beside her, breathing heavily. Her back was to him and his eyes welled with tears.

"I love you, Angela."

She shook her head and reached down for her rumpled clothing. She dressed and was at the door before Red gathered the strength to speak without crying. He rose from the bed, his voice harsh and angry.

"God damn you!"

"I'm sorry," Angela said softly; she left him in the cabin, alone and wanting her.

Red was furious. He'd offered his love, he felt that she'd encouraged him, and he'd been rejected. He'd been kind to her, gentle, soft and slow, even when his nature screamed for him to take her. He'd done everything a man could do.

He snatched his levis from the chair and pulled them on. He rummaged in the dresser drawer for a clean t-shirt and pulled it roughly over his head.

At the bathroom mirror, he examined his face. He was good-looking, his features regular; his red beard framed an honest, impish grin.

There was nothing wrong with him.

He ran his fingers through his hair, remembering the girls he'd seduced in his life. The girls who'd seduced him. The girls who'd told him he was wonderful, an accomplished lover, a damned good catch.

He'd thought that what he'd seen take place between Cynthia and Angela was a part of the possession—now, he wondered if there'd been a possession at all. Perhaps he'd been a pawn of some sort in their bizarre affair.

He'd known some lesbians in his life. They'd griped him,

irritated him, but he never thought of them as dangerous. He knew it was irrational, but he wondered if lesbians *were* witches—if they had some kind of special ESP, some psychic power that allowed them to project images on other people's minds.

He brushed his teeth and followed out the thought.

Perhaps there'd been no ghosts. Perhaps there'd been no possession. Maybe it had been only a strange projection of the women's minds, unleashing a crazy fantasy that had permeated his mind and involved him in their queer relationship. But Abigail, Martha and Squire had once existed. He peered around the door frame and saw the book still lying on the living room floor.

Hell, he thought, they could have gone to a library and looked it up. On the other hand, he wasn't sure a public library would have that information. It had taken his mother years to find a copy. Well, he countered to himself, maybe they *are* witches. Maybe they just *know* things.

The whole thing gave him the creeps.

He rubbed his face dry with a worn towel. He looked at the reflection of his eyes in the mirror. They were slightly bloodshot from crying. He hadn't cried in twenty years, goddammit. Nothing could make him cry.

The look in his eyes became very fierce.

He snapped the lights off in the cabin, stalked to his car, and gunned the engine. Goddamn, he needed a drink.

Cynthia sat up in bed when she heard the downstairs door open, close softly. Footsteps padded up the stairway.

"Angela?"

"It's me," the girl's voice came softly through the hall.

Cynthia signed. "Are you all right?"

There was a silence. Cynthia hurried to the closet, wrapped her robe around her and peered out into the hallway.

Angela stood at the head of the stairs, motionless as a statue. Her eyes were closed and tears streamed down her cheeks. "What am I going to do," she asked, her voice trembling, "What am I going to do? I love you."

"Go to bed, Angela."

Cynthia sat up until she heard the girl's door shut. She

felt as though she'd unjustly punished a child. She knew there was no kind way to reject a would-be lover. Cynthia'd spurned the advances of enough schoolboys and, even after she was married, of local shopkeepers, delivery men and drunken business associates of Dave's to know that rejection always hurt.

Cynthia turned her face into the pillow and wept softly. She hadn't wanted to hurt Angela, but she couldn't see another way. Desperately weary, she let go of all thoughts and her body drifted into a hard, sound sleep.

Angela stood at the window of her bedroom and watched Red's car flash its lights, back up, and head out the main road. From her vantage point, it seemed to be a toy; the man inside it seemed to be a toy, too, a one-dimensional silhouette inside a cracker-jack sized car.

Her thoughts focused on Cynthia. She was flooded with the painful understanding that she'd never lie in those warm arms again. It hurt, oh god, it hurt, but Angela could cry no longer. She saw the single cedar tree swaying at the bottom of the hill. She didn't want to live her life alone.

She undressed then, and slid between the cool sheets. For a moment, she had a wild and frightening forboding. She saw Martha's image in front of her, wrapped in flames, as though it were real. Then, she fell from consciousness, without remembering that she'd neglected to lock the downstairs door.

Chapter Fourteen

The Great Misery Bar and Grill overlooked the bay for which it was named. At midnight, the dinner guests were long gone, and the remaining bar-flys were mostly local boys, heady with their first summer of legal drinking.

"I'm buying this round!" Chip, so called because his jowly young face resembled that of a chipmunk's, waved a five dollar bill at the bored bartender. "Give my buddies here another beer."

"You guys are going to have hangovers tomorrow," the bartender warned as he flushed draft beer into their glasses. "Don't you kids have jobs this summer?"

"I can hold it, man," Chip bragged and slurped the froth from his beer glass. "It's old guys like you who can't keep your liquor down."

The bartender half-grinned and shook his head. "That's the last one that I'm selling you, Chip. I don't want your father down here tearing up my joint because you drove home drunk and wrapped his car around a tree."

"Even ten sheets to the wind, I can outdrive you, old man." The boys with Chip laughed and slapped his skinny shoulders. "Any one of my pals here will vouch for that!"

Red sat at the far end of the bar, staring into his scotch, listening to the locals brag to one another of their mythical exploits.

"There's this whorehouse up in Boston, see," Chip mock-whispered to his friends, "it's out near Fenway Park where all the fags hang out. Well, me and my cousin Ralph went there Easter Vacation. It's got a red light on the door and everything. The chicks were old, man, old, but they still had what we were looking for, so we paid ten bucks. Ralph picked out this black piece of goods. Me, I'm a tit man, so I grabbed this bleached blonde with a chest like this." He made a wide circle with his arms in front of him and the other boys snickered, blowing spitlets of beer from their lips. "Man, she was older than my mother!" The boys broke into guffaws and slapped each other on the back.

Red ordered another scotch and headed for the men's room, stepping carefully over the legs and feet which crisscrossed the aisle. He'd had three double scotches in a row and he was dizzy. He leaned against the sink inside the men's room and tried to vomit, but nothing would come up. He wasn't a drinking man and three double scotches were beyond his limit. He relieved himself, splashed his face with water and returned to the bar to down his fourth.

"Yeah," Chip was continuing, his bravado echoing around the empty bar, "the queers hang out in Fenway Park. They call it the meat rack." He grabbed his crotch to illustrate. "Meat. The meat rack, you get it?" His audience, too drunk to know exactly when to laugh, just stared at him. "Well, my cousin Ralph made out like he was going to go home with one of those queers. Told him that he'd pay him for a blow job. He walked the bastard right to the middle of the park and beat the shit out of him. You shouldda seen it!"

A short boy leaned over and grabbed Chip's arm.

"Beat the shit outta him, huh?"

"Yeah," Chip grinned and rocked back in his chair, "that fag cried like a baby. Ralph broke the bastard's teeth."

"No kidding," the short boy giggled.

"Damned straight."

"Hey," a lean blond boy called across the table to Chip, "you rip off any cigs for us at the supermarket?"

"I got two cartons in the trunk," Chip replied. "Filtered, unfiltered; take your pick." He tossed his car keys to the blond boy.

"I don't know how we're gonna make out when you stop working at the supermarket." The boy grinned, pocketed Chip's keys and jogged toward the parking lot.

"When I get outta law school, I'm gonna buy that fucking supermarket," Chip yelled after him. "I'm gonna be the governor of this fucking state, you'll see."

"I believe you, Chip," the short boy said and sipped his beer.

"I got the brains for it," Chip continued loudly, "and I'm tough enough. That's what counts, you got to be tough. You got to see what you want and take it."

"Damned straight," Red said from the bar.

Chip looked, surprised, at the older man. "Don't ask, take, that's the way to make it in this world. Am I right, man?"

Red's mind was clouded with anger at Angela and too many scotches. He lifted his glass in the air. "Right on," he repeated. He turned to the bartender. "I'm buying this young man a beer."

"He's had enough," the bartender said softly, hoping Chip wouldn't hear.

"For crissakes, I'm nearly twenty years old!" Chip stood and pushed his beer glass across the bartop. "I can handle a couple of beers, for crissakes."

"You betcha," Red agreed.

Chip smiled with pride.

"That's the future of America," Red declared to the bartender as the man reluctantly refilled Chip's glass.

"Dear God," the old man muttered, "I hope not."

Chip seized the beer, took a long gulp, then leaned an elbow on the bar and faced Red.

"Thanks, man."

"Don't mention it."

"You're Richmond, aren't you?"

Red nodded and looked at the boy, puzzled.

"I've seen you with your old lady in the supermarket."

Red smiled. "Yeah. I give my mother a hand. Great lady. She and my Dad are on vacation now."

"No shit? You got a house all to yourself? I wish my folks would take off for a month or so. I still got to make out in the back seat of a car."

"I remember doing that." Red laughed, and slapped Chip's shoulder. "Thank God, those days are gone forever. I've got my own apartment now, in Boston."

"You still in school?"

Red sat up straight. It was an effort, but he didn't like

the implication that he still looked like a college student. "I been out two years."

"No shit? I'll be a freshman in the fall, pre-law."

"That's a tough road to hoe."

"Right." But you can make a killing in it. I couldn't decide for a long time, law or dentistry. With law, I won't have to work so hard and I can still go into politics and make a bundle. Who wants to stare into dirty mouths from 9 to 5?"

"Well, good luck to you." Red turned his attention to his glass. He couldn't think of anything more to say to the kid.

"Listen." Chip leaned against Red's shoulder, buddy-buddy. "We could all drive down to Moorestown, pick up some broads and go to your place. I've got a contact for some grass. Or coke, you name it."

Red shook his head. It made him dizzy. "I don't think so, kid."

Chip smarted at "kid" but he tried not to show it. "Listen," he continued, "I met a neighbor of yours yesterday."

Red raised his eyebrows.

"The blond chick, rented the Rogers house, top of the hill."

Cynthia's face flashed across Red's mind. He hated her, the blond bitch. She'd taken Angela away from him. Bewitched her. If it weren't for Cynthia, he'd be in bed this moment with Angela; she'd be writhing underneath him, begging him to love her, telling him never to stop, giving herself to him. He'd seen the women together in the woods, Cynthia's body where he wanted to be, Cynthia's lips evoking the response in Angela that his maleness should and didn't. It was Cynthia's fault that Angela didn't love him. He hated Cynthia.

He spun to face Chip and nearly lost his balance. Oh Jesus, Red thought, I'm so goddamn drunk. The boy's face blurred and Red blinked his eyes, trying to focus.

"She's some nice piece of ass, huh?" Chip nudged Red in the ribs.

"She's queer." Red spat the words and felt his cheeks flush with rage.

Chip's face opened up with interest. "No shit? I thought the broad was married."

143

"That's the worst kind," Red said furiously, and pounded his fist on the bartop, "she's got a husband and she's shacking up with my girl on the side."

"Your girl?"

Red belched and gripped the bar with one hand, steadying himself. "Damned straight," he said loudly, then dropped his forehead to the bartop and passed out.

Red came to, his head banging gently against the bartop. He felt the pressure of the bartender's gnarled fingers on his shoulders.

"Closing time, buddy. Come on, wake up, it's closing time."

Red forced his eyes open and sat up. He stared at the bartender and wondered where the hell he was.

"You able to drive?" The bartender was looking at him so closely that Red could count the fine lines in the old man's face.

"I'm fine," Red said, and stood up. Gingerly, he removed his hand from the barstool that was supporting him. He lifted one foot and placed it forward. The next thing he knew, he was lying face down on the floor.

"I'll call the cops; they'll drive you home," the old man said. Red tried to look up but the room was spinning. "Next year, for sure, I'm going to retire," the old man mumbled as he walked to the payphone.

"I'll drive him home, Pop." Chip came out of the men's room, zipping his fly. "I go in that direction, anyway."

The old man turned and peered at the boy. "Can *you* drive?"

"You betcher bottom dollar," Chip said manfully, and, slinging one of Red's arms across his own shoulders, he led Red to the silver Eldorado in the parking lot.

"The blind leading the blind," the old man murmured and snapped the padlock on the front door.

Red leaned against his door as Chip's car squealed out of the parking lot.

"Sit up, man, you're going to fall out," the boy said. Red tried, but he could not sit up. "I'm not a drinker," he explained, "I hardly ever drink." He gagged and Chip pulled over to the curb.

"You gonna throw up, do it in the gutter. My Dad'll kill me if you mess up his car."

Red opened the door and leaned out to vomit. He felt better. He slammed the door and sat up straight beside Chip. The world had ceased its spinning, but Red knew that he was still very drunk.

"So you got a lezzie living on the hill?" Chip was eager to open the conversation. He'd had a letch for Cynthia since he saw her in the supermarket.

"Yeah." Red could smell his own foul breath. "Yeah. She's making it with my girlfriend. How'ja like them apples, pal?"

"It sucks, buddy." Chip took a curve, doing sixty-five.

"Je-sus." Red put his hands on his belly as though this would keep him from vomiting again.

Chip laughed. "Listen, you know about lezzies, don't you?"

Red's head was spinning again. He tried to nod.

"They're nymphos." Chip said, with academic authority. "A woman goes queer because she can't find enough men to satisfy her."

In Red's drunken state, he thought it sounded entirely plausible. He nodded, once again.

"If they can't get all the women they want, they start going after little kids, you know that?"

Something about that didn't sound quite right to Red, but his mind wouldn't function. All he could do was keep repeating what Chip said until it sounded true. Chip listened, grinning.

"They get into school systems and girl scout troops, you know, it's really awful. Like a bunch of vampires on the loose. Of course, there aren't really any vampires, but dykes are just about the same thing." Chip talked at random, believing only half of what he said, but enjoying the reaction that his dissertation seemed to have on Red.

"They're that bad, huh?" Red gently laid his head on the back of the seat. He sighed.

"They need a good man to straighten them out. It would be a public service."

Red let his head roll to the side. He looked at Chip and smiled.

145

Chip slapped Red's knee. "You too drunk to do it?"

Red pictured Angela and Cynthia as he'd seen them in the woods. Naked, intertwined, tender and loving. He grew stiff with rage.

"You up to doing a good deed, man?" Chip turned into Richmond Hill Road.

Red sat up, staring at the dark house on top of the hill; he slammed his fist into the padding of the car seat. "You're damned straight I am."

Chapter Fifteen

In her sleep, Cynthia heard the squeal of the car brakes and dreamed that it was Martha's screaming. She felt the searing of the flames against her flesh and woke up suddenly, breathing hard, perspiring.

She threw back the covers, pulled on her robe, and padded barefoot from the bedroom, down the stairs, into the kitchen. She stared beyond it to the old room. She'd hoped that the room was dead, that Martha had, at last, found peace. But now the room seemed to tremble, as it had on the first night. A breeze moved through it, and the timbers shuddered as though in terrified anticipation.

She didn't see the men until they stood behind her, blocking both exits from the kitchen. She opened her mouth to scream, but then she saw that one of the men was Red.

"What's wrong, Red? What are you doing here?"

Red swayed, hands clinging to the doorframe. He grinned broadly.

Cynthia realized Red was drunk. A draft swept through the kitchen. Cold permeated her; she shivered and pulled her robe tightly to her body. Behind her, in the old room, there was a sudden crash. She spun and saw that the sapling chair had toppled to the floor.

"What's the matter, Red?" Cynthia insisted.

Red laughed loudly. Although his eyes were focused on her, they seemed glazed. She wasn't sure that he was seeing her.

She raised her voice. "Red? Red, answer me!"

He laughed again, a guttural sound. His hulking body blocked the doorway to the hall.

Cynthia turned and focused on the stranger who stood in

front of the door that led outside. She knew she'd seen him somewhere before but she couldn't place him.

Chip laughed with bravado.

"Who are you?" Cynthia addressed the boy.

Chip grinned. He half-bowed and said sarcastically, "Just one of your local boy scouts, m'am, come to do a good deed. Always ready to aid a lady in distress."

He unzipped his fly.

Both doors were guarded by the menancing male bodies. Cynthia turned and ran into the old room.

"Come on," Chip ordered Red, "don't go chicken on me now."

Cynthia screamed once, when Chip tore her robe open and shoved her into Red's arms.

"Hold her," Chip hissed, "and keep her quiet, for crissakes."

Red looked with fury at Cynthia.

"It's for her own good," Chip barked.

Red pinned Cynthia's back against his chest. He held her wrists with one hand; his other hand closed tightly over her mouth.

Chip stood in front of her, dodging her kicking feet as though he were playing a game. Then, one of his hands shot out and seized her ankle, throwing her off-balance; she couldn't move. With his other hand, he roughly squeezed her breast.

"It's for your own good," he kept repeating, close to her face. She could smell the beer, and feel the shower of spit each time he spoke.

"You ought to thank me, bitch. I'm going to save your soul."

Chip tried to enter her, but he found the passage blocked. He jammed his fingers in her to locate the obstruction.

"Son of a bitch," he yelled, "God damned bitch has got the curse!"

Cynthia looked straight ahead, but she didn't see Chip. She saw the Elder Richmond strike a match; she saw the smoke that rose from the ignited kindling at her feet; she saw Abigail cry and turn her face away. Red's arms became the bonds that lashed her to the stake; Chip's prying fingers were the flames that ate her flesh.

The scream was ear-splitting.

Red thought, at first, that it had come from Cynthia. Then, he felt fingers tearing at his back and neck. He released his grip on Cynthia, turned to grab Angela's arms and push her to the floor.

He scarcely felt the scratches on his face, he was so wild with lust and liquor. He ripped Angela's nightgown off, and forced her, naked, flailing, underneath him. Then they heard the child's voice from the top of the stairs.

"Mommy! Mommy!"

"Jesus," Chip screamed, staring with horror at his bloodstained fingers, "Why didn't you tell me she's got kids? For crissakes, I didn't know she was a mother!"

"Red sobered suddenly. He pulled himself to his feet.

"Mommy!" the boy cried again.

"I'm getting the hell outta here, man," Chip said. He released his grip on Cynthia, and headed for the back door.

"Hey," Red cried, in panic. "You got us into this! You can't just leave me here."

"The hell I can't," Chip yelled, as he ran from the house.

Red called up the stairway, his voice shaky. "It's okay, Butch, go back to bed."

"Mommy! I want my Mommy!" Red's voice hadn't appeased the boy.

Cynthia pulled her robe tightly around her and raced up the staircase to console her son.

Angela, alone with Red, quickly got to her feet and backed against the wall. Red reached out to her. She cowered.

"I'm so sorry," he whispered.

"Don't touch me."

"I'm drunk. I went crazy with jealousy." He stepped toward her.

She lifted the iron frying pan from the stove and held it to her breasts, as though to shield herself from him.

"I didn't mean to hurt you," Red pleaded. "Don't you understand? I'm in love with you, Angela."

"Don't touch me," she hissed. "I'll kill you if you touch me."

Red saw the hatred in her eyes. He turned, hot tears of shame streaming now from his cheeks; he bolted from the house.

Two uniformed patrolmen arrived shortly after dawn.

It was Cynthia who'd insisted on calling the police. "Dammit," she'd cried at Angela, "we've got rights, too!"

The children, who'd been awake since the screaming began, were playing jacks on the front porch. Their mother had told them that they'd had a prowler in the yard the night before.

"But Mommy scared him off," Janet explained to the policemen, proudly. "He didn't get to steal a thing."

"I'm Lieutenant Sanderson," the portly, older policeman introduced himself. He nodded toward the lean young man who stood beside him. "This is Officer Evans."

Cynthia opened the door. "Come in." The children immediately abandoned their game and rushed to the door. "No," Cynthia said firmly to them, "you wait outside."

The young cop, Evans, leaned against the wall, tapping a pencil against his leather notebook. Sanderson sat on the couch, clearing his throat occasionally, as Cynthia related the events of the night before. She had the feeling that they were barely listening to her.

Angela sat, stoic, in a straight-backed chair across the room. She didn't look at Cynthia.

When Cynthia finished, there was silence in the room. Sanderson cleared his throat again. "The boy in question came into the stationhouse this morning," he said. "He had a feeling you were going to call us, and he wanted us to hear his side of the story. We've known Chip since he was kneehigh. He's the Mayor's son, you know."

"What difference does that make?" Cynthia snapped at the policeman, angrily.

"Hey, take it easy, lady," Evans, the young cop, said.

He closed his notebook and slid it into his breast pocket. He shifted his attention from Cynthia to Angela. He smiled at the pretty, dark-haired girl, but she didn't respond.

"Chip seemed to think you invited him up here," Sanderson stood up and faced Cynthia.

"What?" She cried out.

Sanderson shrugged. "That's what the boy says. He says you came onto him like gangbusters when you were in the supermarket. He's the bagboy there.

"Happens all the time," Evans added. "Women come up here on vacation without their husbands, see a nice-looking young kid . . ." He grinned and winked.

"That's not true!" Cynthia's face flushed with rage.

"I've never known Chip to lie," Sanderson said firmly. "I've known him as I say, since he was kneehigh."

"I've got my rights, too!" Cynthia looked to Angela for support, but Angela stared at the floor.

"Nobody's interfering with your rights, m'am," Sanderson continued. "If you want to press charges, we'll take you to the station right now."

Cynthia reached for her jacket.

"But," Evans said slyly, "you might want to consider the repercussions."

Cynthia already had one arm in her jacket. "Repercussions?"

"Yes, m'am," Sanderson said. "We talked to Richmond this morning, too. He corroborated Chip's story."

"He *what*? Red Richmond wasn't even *at* the supermarket!"

"Oh, not that part, Mrs. Martin." Sanderson quickly looked out the window. "He told us about your quirk."

"Quirk?" Cynthia put her other arm into the jacket and buttoned the top button. "I don't know what you're talking about."

Angela dropped her face into her hands and sighed.

Sanderson's ears were scarlet with embarrassment. He couldn't turn to face Cynthia. "About your liking girls, Mrs. Martin."

Cynthia was so stunned that she couldn't speak.

"Your lesbian activities," Evans elaborated. He clearly found the subject titillating and his eyes darted from Cynthia to Angela and back again. "We figure that you wouldn't want your husband to know about your lesbian

151

activities. Now, if you press charges against Chip and Red Richmond, that will certainly come up in the hearing."

Cynthia sat on the edge of a chair suddenly, as though the wind had been knocked out of her. "I don't understand," she said weakly, "I can't see what *that* has to do with *this*. I was *assaulted*."

Sanderson's voice was soft as he answered her. "It's just your word against theirs, Mrs. Martin. And when they bring that up in court . . ."

"My *quirk*?" Cynthia interrupted sarcastically.

"Yes, m'am. When that's brought up in court, you won't have any credibility. I think it's better, Mrs. Martin, if you just forget that last night ever happened."

"Yeah," Evans added, smiling at Angela. "After all, no one was really hurt."

Chapter Sixteen

Dave arrived at noon. The village taxi (seldom used, in ill repair, and driven, when necessary, by the Methodist preacher's teenage son) dropped him at the front door. The young driver, who'd already heard Chip's expanded version of the previous night's events, insisted on toting Dave's luggage inside so he could get a look at Cynthia. He was disappointed. He'd expected her to look different than other women. She looked like anybody's mother. He was embarrassed, and refused Dave's offer of a tip.

"We had a prowler, Daddy!" Pete clung to his father's legs.

"You don't say?" Dave lifted the boy in his arms, and leaned toward Cynthia to give her cheek a peck.

"Some local nut," she shrugged. "He ran off as soon as we came downstairs and turned on the lights."

"I don't like the sound of that," Dave said protectively. "I'm glad I'm here."

Cynthia put her arms around him and held him hard. "So am I," she said, her head against his.

"Daddy!" Pete said loudly, to be sure his father heard. "I had a yellow dog but it ran away."

"That so?" Dave reached down with one hand and patted his daughter's hair. "You been helping Mommy, honey?"

"I colored a parakeet in purple, blue and green," Janet replied, holding tightly to her father's hand. "You wouldn't think the colors go together, but they do."

Angela prepared lunch in the kitchen while Dave sat with Cynthia on the back steps, watching her paint.

"You've got some imagination, honey," he said, as she filled her charcoal sketch of the old room with splashes of

153

acrylic color. "They didn't use that kind of kettle in the hearth, though; they used a flatter pan, with side handles. I've seen it in the museum."

Cynthia kept painting. "How did the deal go?"

"Continental Coffee?"

She nodded.

He shrugged. "I think they're going to use a name; Paul Lynde, or some damn superstar."

"I'm sorry."

"The kettle's wrong," he repeated, "and the window ought to have some curtains."

He expected her to blot the kettle out, to appease him. He was surprised when she mixed white and grey paint, dipped her brush and put a highlight on the kettle.

He changed subject quickly. "It takes a big agency like Lauder to attract the stars. That's where the money is."

"I'm sure that Mr. Lauder'd like to have you back."

Dave was speechless for a moment; then he exploded. "And lose the money that I borrowed from my mother to start the business? We have to pay that back, you know!"

Cynthia continued painting.

"It's your decision," she said softly, "it's your career."

"Five minutes till lunch," Angela called out the window.

When Dave spotted the old room off the kitchen, he moved directly to it.

"Good God," he said, "look at this!"

Cynthia smiled and nodded.

"I bet this predates the Revolution." Dave wandered into the old room, thumping its siding with his fist. "These beams are handhewn; look at the ax marks. Have you seen this room, honey?"

"Yes, dear, I have."

"Well, did you ask in town about it? I bet somebody in the town knows this room's history. Did you ask at town hall?"

"Your hamburger's getting cold, love."

"You can walk into town hall and ask, you know. That's what they're there for. Where's your curiosity?"

"When you go to town today, why don't you do that?" She smiled at him, and motioned to the hamburger.

154

Dave sat down at the table.

"Two ladies, a boy, and a yellow dog lived in there," Pete said importantly. He nibbled on the bread around his hamburger.

"You don't say?"

"The dog died, Daddy. Somebody killed him."

Dave ruffled his son's hair. "He's got an imagination, too, huh?" He grinned at Cynthia. "I hope this kid doesn't grow up to be an actor."

"I don't like this hamburger," Pete announced. He knew he was the center of attention.

"Shut up, Pete," Janet said. She expected her mother to scold her, but Cynthia smiled at her, instead, and winked.

That afternoon, Dave took the children to see the bay.

Angela sat on the sunporch, watching a mama rabbit herd her youngsters back into their burrow. The front door opened suddenly, and Angela heard Cynthia's voice.

"Angela?"

She turned. It hurt to look at Cynthia. Angela's feelings hadn't changed.

"I'm sorry," Cynthia said softly, not moving toward the girl, "I'm sorry that I've hurt you. I understand the way you feel. I'm flattered, I really am. I love you, Angela, but not the way you love me. I'll understand if you don't want to stay here now. We'll pay your fare back to the city, if you like. I'll tell Dave you're homesick."

"Do you want me to leave?"

"My feelings won't change, Angela."

"Neither will mine," Angela said gently.

"I love Dave and the children. I'm going to try to make my marriage work."

Angela forced herself to reply. "I understand."

"Hey," Cynthia came close and patted Angela's shoulder. "You'll find someone."

"A woman," Angela said, with certainty.

Cynthia smiled. "When love is good, it doesn't matter who the lovers are. We learned that from Martha and Abigail."

Angela nodded, but she couldn't look at Cynthia.

"Love can also be destructive," Cynthia continued softly.

155

"I've learned that, too. Lovers sometimes feed on each other's weaknesses. Dave and I have done that. We've crippled each other with our love."

Angela stared straight ahead and prayed she wouldn't cry until Cynthia was out of sight.

"You remember on the drive up here," Cynthia was saying, "I told you about the Meztek Indians?"

Angela cleared her throat. "They're assigned a space for all eternity."

"Well, Dave and I have been standing on the same space. I have to find my own."

"I wish you luck."

"You, too. You'll find someone, Angela. I know you will."

At that moment, Angela couldn't envision ever loving anyone but Cynthia.

"And when you do," Cynthia squeezed Angela's shoulder, "remember the Meztek Indians, huh?"

Angela held back her tears, and looked up at Cynthia. "I will," she promised, "I'll remember."

After supper, Angela walked to the bottom of the hill.

Red's heart skipped a beat when he saw her standing at the door.

"Goodbye," she said. "I'm leaving in the morning."

Red offered his hand. Angela didn't accept it. "I'm sorry," he apologized again, "so terribly sorry."

"Cynthia's not pressing charges," Angela said softly.

"Thank God for that," Red sighed. "I'm leaving, anyway. I'm going back to Boston."

"Good luck," Angela said; she turned to leave.

Red stopped her with his voice. "Why did you come here? I thought you'd never want to see my face again."

She didn't turn around. Her back to him, she answered, "I know how you feel," she said. "I know how badly it hurts."

Red watched her continue down the hill; he thought that he would love her till the day he died.

Walking up the hill at dusk, Angela saw the yellow flowers by the creek bank. Abigail's flowers. Angela felt warm

suddenly, and safe, as though Abigail were hidden somewhere, smiling at her.

"Goodbye, Abby," she whispered. "Rest in peace."

That night in bed, Cynthia pressed her cheek against the
naked flesh of Dave's broad back. "I love you."

"Me, too," he mumbled sleepily and shifted his weight to
bear the burden of her arm around his waist. "Something
wrong, honey?"

"No."

"You sure? You're acting funny."

"Everything's just fine."

"You haven't been fooling around with some local guy,
have you?"

Cynthia laughed. "You men are all alike. A woman feels
a little happy and you think she's having an affair."

He turned and grinned. "When a man's happy, he *is*
having an affair."

She slapped his buttocks playfully.

"I love you," he said; he shifted his weight again and
snuggled into his sleeping position.

Cynthia stared at the ceiling, watching night shadows
move across each other. She remembered the cardinal rule
she'd learned in art school; when you change a single line,
you change the whole design.

Let go, she thought to herself, let go. Let the children
find their spaces in the world, let Dave have his own.
Somewhere, she'd find a space for herself alone, as sacred
as her soul.

Tomorrow, she would paint a single oak tree.

Downstairs, the old room was still and silent. The sapling chair leaned, broken, in the corner. The ancient bed
frame hugged the wall for support. Only a spider, which
skittered across the blackened hearth, lived in this room
now.

Martha and Abigail were free.

The End

Photo: Beth Allen

JANE CHAMBERS (1937-1983) began her career in the late 1950s as an actress and playwright, working Off-Broadway and in coffeehouse theatre. Her plays have been produced Off-Broadway, in regional theatres, community theatres and on television. She has been the recipient of the Connecticut Educational Television Award (1971/*Christ in a Treehouse*), a Eugene O'Neill fellowship (1972/*Tales of the Revolution and Other American Fables*), National Writer's Guild Award (1973/*Search for Tomorrow*, CBS), the Dramalogue Critics Circle Award and the *Villager* Theatre Award (1981/*Last Summer at Bluefish Cove*), among others. She was a founding member of the New Jersey Women's Political Caucus and of the Interart Theatre in Manhattan, and a member of the Planning Committee of the Women's Program of the American Theatre Association. She was also a member of the Writer's Guild East, the Dramatists Guild, the Author's League, Actors Equity and the East End Gay Organization for Human Rights. On February 15, 1983, she died of a brain tumor at her Greenport, Long Island home; she is survived by her mother, Clarice, her two step-brothers, Henry and Ben, and by her life's companion, Beth Allen. Meridian Gay Theatre has named its International Gay Playwriting Contest in her honor, and the American Theatre Association has created the Jane Chambers Playwriting Award to encourage the writing of new plays which address women's experiences and have a majority of principal roles for women.

ALSO AVAILABLE FROM JH PRESS

Jane Chambers' **LAST SUMMER AT BLUEFISH COVE**
Paperback: (ISBN 0-935672-05-2) $6.95
Special hardcover limited edition; numbered, signed and with an
introduction by the author relating her own experience with
cancer: (ISBN 0-935672-04-4) $25.00

Heralded by audiences and critics alike as the "breakthrough
lesbian play," Jane Chambers' *Last Summer at Bluefish Cove* is
a tender and moving but still hilariously funny portrait of a
tightly knit summer community of long-time lesbian friends.
For one of the women, it is her last summer there, because of
her struggle with terminal cancer. She meets and falls in love
with a woman to whom she can bequeath her special gifts of
warmth, spirit and independence.

> *"A funny, touching, surprisingly upbeat and enlight-*
> *ened portrait of female homosexuality . . . a land-*
> *mark event."*
>
> —OTHER STAGES

Jane Chambers' **MY BLUE HEAVEN** (ISBN 0-935672-03-6) $4.95

The parson comes a-calling on the "Farm Couple of the
Year," Molly and Josie, two lovers who leave sophisticated
Manhattan to rough it in upstate New York, but he finds that
everything's gay in *My Blue Heaven*, Jane Chambers' latest
comedy, written especially for the Second Gay American Arts
Festival, presented by The Glines in June 1981. In two of the
"Adventures of Molly and Jo," a Christian book publisher wants
to publish Molly's fictionalized version of her and Josie's life
together in book form, and later, Molly and Josie are visited
by a childhood sweetheart of Molly's who is now a minister
and wants them to marry to prove how "progressive" he is.

> *"One of the funniest, most life-affirming comedies*
> *to hit New York in the past decade."*
>
> —N.Y. DAILY NEWS